Sarah's Friends Fight Fairy Floss

by
Shona MacDonald

ISBN 978-0-244-07945-1

For Millie and Tessa, I am sorry it's late.

The Fabulous Fairy

'Everyone reads the Fabulous Fairy! Anyone who is anyone is in the Fabulous Fairy and anyone who isn't anyone wants to be in the Fabulous Fairy! If a week goes by without at least one picture of me in it people will think I'm unwell!'

Vanda was angry. She was also very bright but this was because of what she was wearing not because she was angry. As she had explained earlier to Sarah and Emma, bright colours were fashionable for active wear clothes this season. This meant everything was skin tight and in day-glow colours with big, bold patterns. Vanda, who was a six inch tall fairy, was flying round Sarah's bedroom in a distracted state. This gave the girls the feeling that they were watching a large lime green and shocking pink striped beetle try to find its way out of the room. The overall effect was slightly frightening as Vanda was giving off the impression she could sting; or at the very least create panic if she landed in their hair.

'Alright we get it! Everyone reads it and everyone wants to be in it. I still don't know why you're so mad,' said Emma.

Emma had become a friend to Sarah when she had come to visit her Aunt Jane for summer. Emma was nearly nine, a little older than Sarah, and lived with her parents and three brothers in the farm up the road from Sarah's Aunt Jane. Together, the girls had helped return an errant fairy to his family after saving him from being turned permanently into a wood duck when a sea dragon cast a spell on him but that's another story altogether. Anyway, that shared experience brought the two girls close together as they were the only people they knew that could actually see fairies and, let's face it, it isn't the kind of story you share around too much as most people would not believe you.

Sarah had been relieved to be able to share her fairy friends with someone too. Her first encounter with them had been on her own and she ended up rescuing two hundred fairies from a grey dragon on their way to a birthday party. It was an adventure she had had to keep to herself precisely because she knew people wouldn't believe her but now, with Emma being involved with the whole Del duck thing, she had someone who believed her and was on her side. That mattered a lot. They were now a team of sorts and it seemed like their assistance was about to be needed again but they were in the dark as to why as they really couldn't understand why Vanda was so worked up and angry.

'I'm mad because nearly the whole magazine these days seems to be about fairy floss. Nearly half of the pages are advertising the stuff and the other half has photos of people eating it, or pages of recipes for it! It's awful though. Fairy floss is doing terrible things to them and they don't seem to care or even realise,' Vanda was virtually shouting and the girls made calming motions with their hands to settle her down. They didn't want Aunt Jane, or Bertie her dog, to come investigating the noise.

They hadn't seen Vanda this angry before and because she was their friend they were trying hard to listen and sympathise.

'Look we aren't trying to wind you up. We just don't understand why it's such a big deal. You wouldn't happen to have a copy of this Fabulous Fairy with you would you? So we could see what all the fuss was about?' asked Sarah.

Vanda unhooked the gym bag she was carrying - which was co-ordinated to her outfit so was also lime green with big pink stripes - and rummaged around inside producing a small magazine and handing it over to Sarah.

'I'm on page fifteen this week but I'm not happy with the picture at all. Just hold that will you and I'll make it a bit bigger.'

Vanda muttered something so quietly the girls couldn't hear but the magazine started growing until it was a normal size for them to read rather than something they would have needed to read with a magnifying glass. Sarah and Emma sat next to each other on

Sarah's bed and placed the magazine between them. The front cover had a fairy on it eating something.

'That's fairy floss is it? Looks just like candy floss that we get at fun fairs for humans,' said Emma.

'It tastes funny though. It's just sugar and colouring but you can't stop eating it once you've started even though you don't know if you even like it. It's a bit weird really.'

'Yeah, I like it but I think that's because of the texture.' Sarah said. 'You know the way you put it in your mouth and it sort of dissolves into nothing? Then you have to try again just to see if it'll do the same thing and before you know it this big pink cloud of sugar has become a tacky mess stuck to a wooden stick and you don't know if you want more of it because you don't feel like you've eaten anything or if you just want to be sick.'

'Yes that's it exactly!' Vanda exclaimed. 'It's horrible stuff. It always makes me feel sick when I try it and now I just don't bother. I don't see the point of it.'

'This is what you're all worked up about? I still don't understand,' said Emma.

'Well do you eat it every day? Do you eat it more than once a day? Do you crave it all the time and never shut up about it?' Vanda asked the girls.

'Well of course not!' said both Emma and Sarah.

'I don't think I'd want to eat it every day and my mum certainly wouldn't let me,' said Emma.

'Mine neither,' said Sarah. 'You only get that kind of stuff when you go to fun fairs so it's not that often you get the chance to eat it.'

'It's the same for us. Well kind of,' said Vanda settling down a little and shouting less. 'You see we can't pick and choose when we have it as normally you can only get fairy floss twice a year. It's a treat really unless you're like me and you can't stand the stuff. I suppose it's a bit like having two Easters in a year and getting chocolate eggs then but at no other time. It means some people go a little bit crazy and eat as much as they can when it's available

3

because they know they won't be able to get it again for quite a while when it's gone.'

Vanda took a deep breath and made sure the girls were paying attention to her before she continued. 'Something has changed. Someone has figured out how to make fairy floss all year round it seems and so people are eating it but they aren't being sensible. They are eating it like it's a treat that's going to go away soon so they'd better eat as much of it as they possibly can now while they still can!

'And why is this such a problem?' asked Sarah as the two girls continued to flick through the pages of the magazine.

It was surprising how similar it was to human magazines. There were lots of photos of presumably famous - or important - fairies doing things, there was a section on recipes which admittedly seemed to involve putting fairy floss on top of everything and there was even a horoscope page and some puzzles next to it.

'You look good I think Vanda,' Sarah said turning the pages back to where Vanda had said she was featured.

'Because,' said Vanda in the exasperated tones of a parent talking to a child who wasn't seeing the really obvious thing in front of them. 'Because it's making them sick! Look at these people! Look at those people next to me in that photo! I look tiny compared to them and a couple of weeks ago we were the same size. They are eating way too much of this stuff and its making them put on lots of weight and they aren't healthy. None of them look healthy to you do they? Their skin is bad; you can see from the amount of make-up Sivle is wearing in that photo that he's trying to hide spots. Tarby? You see Tarby in the background? Well he's normally my workout partner at the gym. Does he look like someone that goes to the gym? I haven't seen him for a week! I just can't get him to come and do any exercise anymore and he's putting on a tonne of weight and he's become really grumpy too. No one is acting normal anymore and it's got to stop before something bad happens to one of them.'

4

'I kind of see your point now you mention it. I don't see how we can help. I mean we can't exactly tell fairies what to eat and what not to eat, we aren't experts, and if they aren't listening to you as their friend what can we be expected to do?' Emma asked. 'We don't even know if its fairy floss that's the cause either,' she added.

'Oh I've already given up trying to get them to stop eating the stuff. That's just not going to happen I can tell. What I want you to help me with is stopping them being able to get the fairy floss in the first place!' Vanda replied agitatedly.

'Hang on,' said Sarah. 'You mean to tell me that you've decided to control what they can all eat by taking their choices away from them? That doesn't sound right to me at all. That's just meddling with their lives. It'll only cause trouble.'

'Are you telling me that your parents have never told you that you have to eat all your vegetables before you get a pudding? Do you always get to choose exactly what you want to eat and would you want the same thing all the time if you could?' Vanda asked.

'Well no,' replied Sarah. 'Not exactly but everyone knows that you can't have what you want all the time. I can't eat just chocolate and ice cream can I? It'll make me sick. Even I know that. What is it they say?'

'Everything in moderation,' said Emma interrupting her. 'Everything in moderation my mum says. That way sometimes you get to have the things you know aren't that good for you as a treat. I think most people understand that you can't have what you want all the time don't they? I mean my mum is the most amazing baker, everyone knows that, but she doesn't feed us her cakes and biscuits for dinner. We eat the sensible stuff too like vegetables,' said Emma. 'Mind you my older brothers say they hate carrots and Ben, my little brother, gags when mum makes him eat Brussel sprouts.'

'Exactly my point,' said Vanda. 'Everyone knows they can't have everything they want all the time. It's just right now it seems that my fairies don't. They are acting like they just don't care. Some are eating only fairy floss! Imagine that! Breakfast, lunch and dinner that nasty sugary icky stuff! They have forgotten the 'everything in moderation' rule. I have to take some kind of action because I don't know what else to do.'

'It's also quite possible that they've all been enchanted,' she said darkly lowering her voice and waggling her eyebrows.

Vanda went back to flying distractedly round the room as her thoughts started bubbling up from inside trying to escape.

'I don't know how exactly though. I mean fairy floss used to be a twice a year treat and now it's everywhere. You can't stop them buying it, you can't open a magazine without seeing it, and everyone is acting like its normal. Seems like classic enchantment kind of stuff to me. I bet you there's someone behind all this deliberately getting them to eat this stuff. They must know what damage they're doing but whoever they are they just don't care.'

'Umm,' said Emma quietly so as not to agitate Vanda. 'I think possibly that you're maybe going too far? What would be the point of making all the fairies sick through over eating fairy floss. What does that achieve?'

'I don't know do I!' Vanda screeched in frustration and she flew round in a tight spiral of concentration before blurting out. 'You must know that fairies get banished occasionally? I bet you anything that someone that's been banished has come back to wreck havoc on the clan after years wandering alone in the wilderness!' Vanda replied.

'Well that's just flat out melodramatic,' replied Emma. 'You can't seriously think up some daft idea like that and expect us to believe it. Why create a disgruntled wicked fairy to come back and get you all to eat yourselves to death. That sounds just plain fanciful to me. What do you think Sarah?'

Sarah took a moment to think about what the other two had just said before replying.

'I admit it sounds completely far-fetched. A banished fairy comes back and persuades fairies to eat themselves to death. You'd think there would be an easier way to get your own back if you really were that way inclined. But at the same time I'm no real expert on fairies and I guess they are probably just like us. There may well be some bad guy lurking in the background ready to make everyone's life miserable and this is the way they've decided to do it. I really don't know. Come to think of it we've got an old fairy tale about a witch and a gingerbread cottage that has some similarities. I reckon that if people have enough time and motivation on their hands they can dream up some mad idea and probably make it happen.'

'So you'll help me then?' Vanda asked. She seemed suddenly so much more positive now that they were taking her seriously.

'Truthfully I don't know how,' replied Sarah. 'I mean obviously we would help if we thought we could. However, I doubt a couple of humans turning up and telling everyone to stop eating so much fairy floss would achieve anything.'

'If I can get proof that there's someone behind this? That there is a reason this is happening then will you help me?' Vanda asked with a note of pure desperation to her voice.

'Well of course. If we can we will,' said Sarah. 'Anyway you said it was advertised in the magazine. Who's doing the advertising? Is there a name of a fairy there that's selling the stuff?'

Emma picked up the magazine and sorted more carefully through its well thumbed pages until she got to a one-page ad for fairy floss. 'It says here to contact Gula for *The Most Fabulous and Finest Fairy Floss.* They've even used capital letters. Do you know who Gula is Vanda?' Emma asked.

'Well no. I don't read the adverts for something I don't like do I,' Vanda responded. 'It's strange though that I don't recognise the name at all. I thought I knew everyone who was anyone. By now I would have thought that someone who is that well-known for their product should have bumped into me at some social function or another. You girls leave it to me though. I will find out exactly who they are and what they are about.'

Emma looked puzzled, 'How do you make fairy floss? Humans make it in big metal drums that spin sugar out really fast and you wind it onto sticks and then eat it. But it's all machinery. I guess you guys don't use machinery to make it do you? Is it just magic?'

'Oh no of course not. Magic doesn't make things it can only change things that are already there. Big metal drums huh? That sounds really quite odd. No, as I said it's seasonal it's made from the silk of a spider that shows up here twice a year and then moves on,' replied Vanda.

Emma and Sarah looked at each other in astonishment.

'You eat spider silk and it tastes like sugar?' Emma asked.

'Yes. It's a very natural product compared to what you describe which just seems a weird way to make food to me. Apparently the taste of it changes depending on what the spiders have been eating.'

'The two girls thought about what spiders ate and what that meant the fairy floss tasted like. For starters it didn't sound like it would be strawberry flavoured.

'But you say it's sugary?' Emma wasn't letting go of this, she wanted to understand. 'I thought spiders ate flies and things. How could their silk possibly be sugary if they eat flies?'

'Because they don't all eat flies. Some of them take nectar from flowers. Some spiders are vegetarian I think, I was told that anyway. That's why I said we only normally get the stuff twice a year. You don't get it from just any old spider you know. And it's not normally available in such great quantities either. It used to be that you'd get a little bit to share around the family as it was so expensive and was only intended as a little treat; not a main part of the meal. Now though you can get huge great big bags of it and it's so cheap it really doesn't make sense. I mean I've never seen one but I've been told the spiders are quite small and they only produce a small amount of the silk. They aren't harmed in anyway either, the silk is taken once the spider isn't using it anymore.'

'So where exactly is it all coming from?' Emma asked. 'It doesn't make any sense to me Vanda. I think you need to do a little

8

more research before we can talk sensibly about what our options are.'

'I think you're right now I'm thinking clearer,' said Vanda. 'It's just that I've had no one to talk to about this and so all I've been doing is worrying as things get worse and worse. I feel better for having someone listen to me but you're right, I need to find out more before we can decide what to do. Thank you girls I must get back now. I hope to have something for you very soon.'

Vanda disappeared abruptly, as she normally did, but not before planting a kiss on each of the girl's foreheads on her way.

Emma and Sarah sat in silence once their friend had gone. Neither knew what to say. Spider silk was candy floss apparently, and it didn't taste of flies either.

'Well I'm sure she will be back soon,' said Sarah. 'There isn't a gossip network Vanda isn't plugged into. She'll find out who this Gula person is in no time.'

Emma was still flicking through the pages of the Fabulous Fairy magazine that Vanda had left behind.

'You'd better hide this in case your Aunt Jane see's it Sarah and give it back when Vanda shows up again. I wouldn't want to explain this to your Aunt if she finds it.'

The two girls had a good look through it before Emma had to go back home and Sarah hid it under the mattress. That evening both girls went to bed thinking about what Vanda was up to and Sarah had a dream about a giant spider with big glowing green eyes eating strawberries.

Tattle and Saphia

The next time the girls saw Vanda she had company with her. Sarah and Vanda both had small crystals that had been given to them by the fairies. These had some magical properties; one of which was that the fairy that gave you the crystal would know where you were when you carried it with you. Sarah had been given her crystal by Vanda while Emma's was a gift from Ferric and his family (his brother Del was the one they had rescued from becoming a duck). So when Sarah and Emma, who were playing in the fields owned by Emma's family at Fawcett's Farm, were suddenly interrupted by the appearance of these two fairies they were not especially surprised as it had happened before. What they were not ready for was how Ferric would look nor the presence of an extra couple of fairies they didn't know.

Ferric was tall for a fairy at almost eight inches. He wore camouflage fatigues because he had worked in security before joining his brother in his new business of byssus cloth production. This change had come about as a result of the girls' last adventure. They knew him to be a strong and fit fairy but now he seemed flabby and carrying a little too much weight. His clothes appeared tight across his chest and stomach and he didn't look at all well. They couldn't believe how quickly he had changed from the fairy they had seen at a gala dinner dance less than two weeks ago into the fairy in front of them now.

The other two fairies looked a lot more like Vanda. One of them was slimmer but much more toned and muscled than Vanda, so as she hovered next to Ferric, it emphasised his lack of fitness and how big he was. She also wore almost the same outfit as Vanda; more gym gear. Vanda wore a leotard and tights with a big yellow star over her stomach that radiated orange light in a background of red while this new fairy had a green star that radiated turquoise light on a background of purple. They were quite shocking outfits truthfully but the girls said nothing to be polite. The other new fairy was

10

similar in size to Vanda and while still in her gym clothes she had stuck with tried and trusted black with black on black. Everything about her was black including the shoes.

'Ladies! So lovely to see you and I hope you don't mind I brought some friends along too? Vanda said before launching into her introductions.

'Of course you already know Ferric. So this is Tattle,' she indicated the taller, brighter fairy. 'She is the instructor of our F18 class and the absolute best in the business if you want a strong core and awesome legs. She is simply a marvel.'

'Hello girls! Wonderful to meet you both! I do hope we are going to be the best of friends! I have been so dying to meet you as Vanda says the most lovely things about you both and I am so happy to finally get to meet you!'

Tattle smiled the biggest, brightest smile the girls had ever seen and watched as she flitted between them and Vanda so fast it was like watching a hummingbird. She somehow managed to sound even more enthusiastic than Vanda. You could almost hear the exclamation marks dropping into place when she spoke.

'Saphia,' Vanda indicated the other fairy in black, 'and I went to school together and we have been best friends forever. She does something to do with history. I can never remember what it is exactly but it's awfully impressive I do know.'

Saphia rolled her eyes at this, 'I'm actually a social anthropologist. I study how similar, and different, societies are. Nice to meet the pair of you. I had heard Vanda had been travelling a more unconventional path when it came to friends of late, not that I'm judging you because you're human of course.'

She didn't busily flit around like Tattle but remained exactly where she was successfully giving off the impression that none of this was her idea, she wasn't impressed, and she'd only come along because it was easier to give in to Vanda than argue with her.

'Is this going to take long? Only I have a lunch organised with the weavers to celebrate the success of the byssus fabric and apparently I need to make a speech,' asked Ferric.

Emma and Sarah were staring at him and it was clearly making him uncomfortable.

'Are you okay Ferric?' Emma asked. 'Only I don't remember you looking so pale before and...' her voice trailed off as she tried to think of a polite way of saying it looked like he'd put on a lot of weight and didn't look very well before she gave up. Ferric seemed completely oblivious to this awkwardness. It was like he didn't care if he was there or not. He had always been quite quiet, but then most people were quiet compared to Vanda, but he just didn't seem right at all.

Vanda stepped in to rescue the situation. 'I'm sure you don't need to stay at all if you don't want to Ferric. It was very kind of you to come along because I needed to know if the girls were together and you're the one tuned in to Emma's crystal. As it seems to be a ladies gathering anyway and I'm sure if you need some time to work on your speech you'd better go. Thanks for your help. I really appreciate it.'

And with that he vanished, with a quick 'Goodbye and nice to see you again.'

'I told you didn't I?' Vanda was looking at Emma and Sarah who were still looking at the space where Ferric had been.

'How has that happened so fast? How can he possibly have put on all that weight so quickly? And how has he let that happen? He is so conscious of his health and fitness.'

The shock was obvious in Sarah's voice and Emma's face. They really hadn't been expecting such a massive change in someone they knew in such a short space of time.

'I suspect fairies are different to humans and so we gain weight, and likely lose it, faster than humans.' Saphia said in a voice that somehow reminded both girls of their scariest teacher at school. It was a voice to be listened to.

'Our metabolisms are different. The way we use and store food is different. From what I've observed of this phenomenon so far it seems clear that a massive increase in calories from sugar with a complete halt in exercise produces an exceptionally rapid weight gain in fairies. Of course we'll need to study this a little longer before we can reach any valid conclusions.'

Emma and Sarah stared open-mouthed at the fairy in black waiting to see what she would say next. They didn't want to say anything themselves in case it was wrong, as they both had the feeling they would get lines to write as punishment if it was.

'Oh don't mind Saphie,' said Vanda. 'She smarter than everyone I know and you just get used to it after a while. She's quite brilliant really it's just that the rest of us can't keep up. Right now though I am quite up to speed and completely agree with her. Fairies are putting on weight really, really fast and all of us here think it's the fairy floss. You've just seen the evidence with Ferric. It's all he seems to eat these days.'

Sarah and Emma sat in the grass in the field. Bertie, Aunt Jane's collie dog, was charging around the field chasing sea gulls and was paying the girls no attention. Sarah was always a little concerned when Bertie and fairies were together at the same time. She was pretty sure he wouldn't try and eat one but he might damage one no matter how fast they were and she was always wary of what might happen.

'You mean to tell us that since the gala Ferric has suddenly put all that weight on and it's down to fairy floss alone?' Sarah asked.

'Why is it that you three don't seem to be showing the same signs? We know that Vanda doesn't like fairy floss but how about you two?'

Tattle was the first to respond. She seemed positively bursting with enthusiasm to speak.

'I couldn't possibly even consider eating that stuff. It's so bad for you don't you think? My job and reputation is all about health, I am expected to set the best example, to be the fittest and strongest and I take that very seriously! If people come to my classes to train I can't be setting a bad example. I need to be what they can aspire to be in terms of healthy living! I can't be seen out at parties, eating food that's bad for you, staying out late. It's harder than you think being this perfect. It takes effort and commitment and very few appreciate the time I put into it! The hours in the gym by myself, the perfecting of techniques, the training schedules I create for others...'

'I think we get the idea Tattle,' said Saphia butting in to save them from an extensive lecture. 'I didn't know what was going on until Vanda told me at the gym. I don't get out of my study often except to meet her or other researchers so didn't even realise fairy floss was available so I haven't become like the others and before you ask no I don't intend to having seen the consequences. The reason I have decided to take an interest is because this could be a unique opportunity to study how a society breaks down or evolves. Who knows which? I am going to observe and record this behaviour not meddle in it. I believe Vanda wishes to meddle however and heaven forbid I try and change her mind.'

Saphia seemed to have finished so Vanda took her chance to fill the silence.

'Emma and Sarah you are looking at the only three fairies I could find who aren't enchanted by fairy floss,' Vanda exclaimed triumphantly.

'Are you still thinking this is an enchantment? It just seems like a food fad with bad consequences to me,' said Sarah.

'Well whatever,' replied Vanda, who was managing to flounce in mid air and give off the impression of being terribly hurt.

'I know what I think and as Saphie says we will observe and then we'll see who's right. Anyway, that's not what today was about. I wanted us to meet today because we've found something out about this Gula person we talked about.'

Saphia produced a black notebook from a black bag she was carrying and opened it. The girls couldn't read what was written inside, as it was too small, but Saphia's teacher voice made up for that.

'Gula appears to have been outcast from our clan many years ago and in unusual circumstances. At the time Gula was a child, less than twenty years of age. The incident involved her parents who by all accounts we're gifted farmers. They were floss farmers of the biannual, or twice a year, spider silk harvest we also know as fairy floss. It seems they were cast out when they were asked to keep the spiders longer than they would normally because a particular family, the name is not shown in the records, wanted a large amount for a wedding that was going to happen a month after the fairy floss season was over. Gula's parents refused. It seems that whoever wanted the floss was rather important and they pulled a few strings and basically had the whole family thrown out of the clan.'

'It's all really rather shocking and blatantly wrong. The family were trying to do the right thing and they got punished for it. Normally if banishment is being considered a session of the elders and peers is convened because it is a final binding decision and so needs to be discussed openly and fully to see if it really is the appropriate action. These meetings are usually recorded but I cannot find any record of this one in our libraries and can only therefore assume that it did not happen. Whoever had this done was powerful enough to make it happen without the rest of the clan knowing,' Saphia paused.

'I suppose that being banished is forever right?' Emma asked. 'I mean you don't get banished for a year or ten years. It's permanent yes?'

'Absolutely, there is no coming back if you are an adult,' replied Saphia. 'However in the case of Gula things are different. She was only nineteen years old. You are not considered an adult until you are fifty years of age. In such circumstances, when the child leaves with the parents, there is the possibility of the child returning to the clan but it rarely happens.'

'Well that's hardly surprising is it,' said Vanda. 'I mean really. Would you want to come back to a clan that had treated your family so poorly? Wouldn't you just stay away and start a new life somewhere else? It just doesn't make sense to come back. Not if you're carrying that kind of emotional baggage.'

'Oh I don't know. I think it takes a strong brave person to come back. I wonder what happened to her parents?' This comment came from Tattle who was doing pull ups using the lower branch of a small hawthorn tree nearby.

Saphia sighed, 'We don't know. They'd been banished and for all we know they could still be alive. Gula may have chosen to leave her parents and come back to us on her own. She is nearly seventy years old now. She can make her own decisions. I'm sure whatever has happened to her life has not been easy.'

Tattle did a perfect back flip off the branch she was holding, landed lightly on her feet and then jogged, rather than flew, back to the others.

'Agreed but if she came back to get even and wanted to find whoever was responsible why not do just that? Then she could have had it out with them and got it resolved. I mean no one is mean enough to take out their anger and frustration on people who didn't even know about the banishing anyway?' Tattle smiled beautifully at them all. Her brow was furrowed as she tried to imagine someone doing something so horrid. Clearly she didn't think someone could ever be so mean.

'I hate to give you bad news,' said Emma. 'But people are more than capable of making others suffer who never did anything wrong to them. I'm sure Saphia knows enough about the similarities between humans and fairies to say that the same applies.'

'Unfortunately you are correct Emma, humans and fairies are similar in many ways. Pointless suffering is caused all the time. For example the wrong thing said at a wedding can cause families to feud for hundreds of years even when they've forgotten why.'

16

Sarah was chewing a piece of grass and listening to the conversation. She didn't feel like Gula was going to be an easy problem to solve. She actually felt sorry for her.

'Trying to see it from her point of view is just too hard. I think that going to her directly and accusing her is just wrong. We don't know for certain that she's behind this. For all we know she could be being used by someone else. What if her parents are still alive and they've sent her back to cause this damage on their behalf, for their revenge, and she doesn't want to do it? Imagine how conflicted she must be.'

'I think trying to persuade the fairies to stop eating fairy floss, or eat less of it, is the first thing we have to try. Otherwise we potentially make Gula's life harder than it's already been,' said Tattle. 'And I have just had the best idea as to how. We are going to hold a good old fashioned Highland Games! We used to have them but no one has organised one in ten years or so! With my fitness knowledge and Vanda's organising abilities it'll be easy!' she beamed at them sure in the knowledge of the brilliance of her brainwave.

Saphia noisily cleared her throat, or maybe laughed, it was hard to tell.

'I was just getting to you Saphie darling! You'll be the Chief Referee and Holder of the Records! If anyone can find the results from the last Highland Games it'll be you. The way I see it if we can persuade the fairies to try and re-live their sporting prowess of ten years ago and they see that they can't come even close because of their weight gain and fitness loss it'll wake enough of them up from this fairy floss coma to stop them eating it!'

Once again the exclamation marks were almost audible as Tattle's enthusiasm gushed over them. It was hard to say no to someone with such a positive attitude but Saphia tried anyway.

'I really don't have time for this you know. You don't need someone like me there are plenty of others who can do the job,' she tried.

'No Saphie it has to be you! No one can do it better than you and anyway you're one of the few who hasn't been affected by all this nonsense. And it'll be such fun, us girls together doing this for everyone, you simply have to!'

Saphia knew better than to continue arguing in the face of such crazy keenness so she nodded her consent and gave in gracefully.

'Well good luck with that,' said Sarah. 'Obviously we'd love to hear how it turns out. Do let us know won't you.'

'Oh I think not Sarah and Emma. I do believe you will make fabulous guest judges! After that gala you attended, and once the talk about Vanda's stunning dress had died down a little, you two became the talk of the town. You were sat with Princess Salix and everyone wants to know more about you but they were too polite at such a formal event to be nosey. If the idea of reliving their previous athletic prowess isn't enough to motivate them then being nosey about you two certainly will. Fairies are terrible gossips and this way we make sure they will come.' Tattle was quite pleased with her idea and Sarah and Emma felt trapped just like Saphia who seemed to be quietly laughing at them.

'You'll also get to see the full scale of the problem,' said Vanda. 'This way you'll really see what a mess she's made in such a short time. You won't be able to pretend you don't know what's happening.'

Sarah and Emma knew there was no point arguing against both Vanda and Tattle and, truthfully, they were both more than a little curious about the state of the fairies having seen Ferric.

'Face it Sarah,' said Emma. 'Who gets to judge a fairy Highland Games? Of course we'll do it. Just tell us when and where. We're in.'

'A Highland Games won't take long at all. Let's say the day after tomorrow?' said Vanda 'I mean we already have the equipment it just needs setting up and I'm thinking the less time we give people to think about this the better. Use their initial enthusiasm and bravado before they've had a chance to really think it through properly.'

'But how will people get to know about it? That's no time at all.' asked Sarah.

'My dear girl! I thought you knew me better than that by now,' said Vanda. 'I can have the whole place know by later this afternoon! Word-of-mouth and a couple of posters - especially with your names on - and we may need to use a bigger venue than normal. No come to think of it I'll use my trick from the Gala maybe? What do you think Saphie darling?'

Vanda had had a brilliant idea last time the girls had needed to visit the fairies underground. She had used a spell on the room that she normally used on her handbags that always seemed to contain so many things. What it did was expand the inside of the space temporarily. She had discovered it could be applied to rooms as well as bags. The supplier of the spell had been quite impressed. He'd never thought of it himself and it had made for an extremely grand space for the dinner and dance.

'I think we'd be better off having it outside at the old quarry on the north side of the farm Emma's family have. No one ever goes there, including the sheep, as it's all fenced off and we can just put an anti-weather dome spell over the top of it as I'm sure it'll be raining. It's always raining,' replied Saphia.

'Oh! It'll make it more rugged and outdoorsy! I love it!' Tattle had been distracted while this had been going on. She had found two small stones roughly the same size and appeared to be doing weight training with them.

'Come on ladies! No time to lose! We have to make a start if this is going to happen. It was so lovely to meet you finally! Just wait till my afternoon class hears about this!' said Tattle and she promptly vanished.

'Is she always like some kind of energiser bunny?' asked Sarah.

'I have no idea what an energiser bunny is Sarah but if you mean is she always on the go, always doing something and impossibly happy all the time then yes; she's just like one of your bunnies,' said Saphia who was placing the folder back in her bag and looked like she what going to go too.

'A trip to the library for me I think. At least I know where I'll be able to find the results from last time. We are a terribly competitive lot so there is no way they'll have gone missing so my job is pretty easy and anyway as Ferric's dad runs the library I shouldn't have to search hard at all,' and she too vanished.

Ferric's dad, Barum, was a librarian and an exceptional cataloguer of books. The girls had met both him and his wife, Aurum, when they had had the unfortunate responsibility of telling them about their other son, Del, being turned into a duck by a sea dragon. It had been a strange couple of days but things had eventually worked out okay.

'I'd best be off too Emma and Sarah. Looks like I'll see you in a couple of days. You know where the old open quarry is Emma? I'm sure your mum and dad have told you to keep away from it but don't worry. It'll be safe for the day. I'll see you both there bright and early around eight in the morning? That way you can watch everyone arrive so do be prepared for a shock. You've both seen quite a lot of fairies now and very few of them look the way they should do. I can't stress that enough,' said Vanda before vanishing after the other two leaving Sarah and Emma alone again.

Sarah called Bertie the dog to her. He was still chasing birds in the field and the two girls began the walk back to the Fawcett's Farm.

'So what do you make of all that?' Emma asked Sarah as they navigated a gate remembering to close it carefully behind them.

'I mean Ferric looked terrible. Vanda is quite melodramatic but her heart is in the right place. I'm quite curious to see how they look at the Games and if they really are all as bad as Ferric. If they are I think we need to try and help somehow if we can. If they are similar to us then putting on all that weight won't be healthy will it? I just hope it doesn't come to that,' replied Sarah.

As they got back to the farm Emma's return was announced by the excited yapping and barking of the farm dogs who were related to Bertie. The doggy family reunited briefly before Sarah called Bertie away from the group and headed back down the rutted road to her Aunt Jane's cottage.

The Highland Games

The day before the games seemed to take forever for both of the girls as they couldn't wait to see what would happen. What exactly went on at a fairy Highland Games? Did they have the same events like tossing the caber that a human Highland Games would have? Both Sarah and Emma were up and out early that day having made up an excuse about spending the day in the hills together. They rendezvoused at the farm so Emma could take Sarah to where the quarry was as she hadn't been there before as it was generally understood to be out-of-bounds.

There they found Vanda waiting just as she'd promised.

'I tell you this is going to be such fun. I can't think why we stopped having these games I really can't. Tattle has gone all out, she has even invented a new event too although I'm not sure what everyone will think of it. It's a circuit of different exercises that you have to do as fast as possible. She's calling it Racing Round. I've got no idea if anyone will enter as it looks quite hard. Virtually no one is here yet as we wanted to make sure you two had a good spot with plenty of space and that we could then organise equipment around you for the events.'

Vanda had chosen a very natty outfit for the day. It made her look a bit like a tennis umpire. She had on a smart blazer in dark blue with a white shirt and blue and white tie. She also wore a beautiful white pleated skirt and flat white shoes. The overall effect was finished off with a straw boater hat with a blue and white ribbon round the top. It was the most conventional looking thing the girls had ever seen her in and they had to comment.

'Oh it's a uniform really. Everyone who is officiating will be wearing the same outfit that way it's obvious who's in charge and who is competing,' Vanda told them.

She flew ahead of the girls and they had to walk fast to keep up as they approached the old quarry.

'Now don't you girls worry about a thing. Saphie has been a marvel and got on to the team that normally do tunnel works. They've fixed up a weatherproof invisible ceiling and no-one will be able to see us inside either. To passing humans it will look just like an empty quarry. I am told it was all rather easy. This team are so used to factoring in keeping earth and rocks from crashing down that just keeping back a bit of sky was a doddle. I think they are enjoying the change and some of them are staying around to compete,' Vanda told them.

The girls got to an old rusty barbwire fence and squeezed their way through it making sure not to get their clothes caught. They cautiously followed Vanda down the slope as they were now walking on the very edge of the quarry that dropped down on their left-hand side. When they got to the base of the hill they turned to look in at the old quarry. The top, where they had squeezed through the fence, was maybe fifteen meters above them and it was twice as wide as it was tall. It was quite small and the girls could tell it was old. The rocks that had once been exposed fresh and clean were now covered in moss and lichen. Grasses, and even a few hardy trees, grew in the narrow spaces where roots could get a hold between the cracks in the rock. The floor was covered in grass and moss with a few stone lumps lying abandoned in disorganised heaps.

'Looks like we're here first,' said Emma.

'Oh no absolutely not,' replied Vanda and she waved her hand in front of her and told the girls to step forward three paces with their eyes closed. They did as she asked and after the second step they both heard a small popping noise in their ears. On the third step they opened their eyes and what they saw wasn't what they had just been looking at.

Instead of an old quarry it was a great amphitheatre. The back wall, that had looked so old and worn seconds ago, was now covered with flags of many colours filling every little crevice and crack. Seats were somehow perched on every available rock ledge. A narrow gap had been left down the middle, between all the flags and furniture, which appeared to be a climbing wall. The floor of the quarry was littered with pieces of equipment. Some looked sort of familiar from school and some were less obvious. In front of the girls a small group of fairies had gathered to meet them all dressed the same way as Vanda. Most of them they had met before but Vanda felt the need to let them know who was in charge of what anyway.

'Sarah and Emma I'd like to introduce you to the six hundred and forty sixth Highland Games organising committee! Tattle, who you have already met, is the Chief Official and her word will be final in the case of disputes. Saphie darling is of course in charge of recording the illustrious achievements of our competitors today and Sivle has done an amazing job with the refreshments available for spectators and competitors alike and has managed to find something other than fairy floss after I told him our partnership was over if he didn't.'

Vanda smiled sweetly at her business partner Sivle who, the girls had to admit, was also looking a little – to be polite - heavier and paler than when they'd last seen him. Vanda and Sivle seemed to organise all the events and parties and they must be very busy as the fairies seemed to have an awful lot of them.

'Lovely ladies it is a real pleasure to see you again and we really appreciate you taking time out to come and help us here today,' said Sivle.

'We have key roles for you with regard to the rock climbing competition as well as the piping event which will be hotly contested I can tell you.' He took off his boater hat and held it in front of him, suddenly looking rather guilty and nervous.

'In fact, to be completely honest with you, the reason you're officiating the piping event is because it has in the past come to blows between the competitors and judges. This way we figured no one will argue if the judges are a hundred times bigger than the competitors and, we hope, that your word will indeed be final when it comes to who has won for a change.'

'Piping? Do you mean like bagpipes?' Sarah asked. 'I'm not sure either of us knows the first thing about bagpipes or whether they sound good or not.'

'No. These aren't the bagpipes they are rock pipes. It's a rather tricky instrument,' replied Sivle.

'The player needs to be immensely strong to lift the pipes which, as the name suggests, are made of rock. The hollow pipes are strapped together in groups of three meaning it requires speed to switch quickly between groups of pipes whilst playing and they need a lot of puff to blow them to make any noise at all. It's not an instrument many learn as any child as you need a lot of strength and we don't make smaller versions for children. As you can imagine the fairies capable of playing are bigger than most and judging the contest is not for the faint-hearted. If a player feels he was better than the overall winner there's nothing quite as disconcerting for a judge, and I know because I have been one, as the thought of an irate pipe player living close by and what he could do to you. In fact I owe you a personal debt of gratitude for volunteering for this role as otherwise I would have had to do it again.'

'I'm really not sure we're qualified for the role though,' said Emma, turning to Sarah for her support.

'I think she's right Sivle. We have no idea what these things sound like never mind if the player is any good. We're bound to get it wrong,' replied Sarah.

She looked down to Sivle and could see that he was devastated by this. In fact his shoulders were starting to shake and it looked like he could possibly burst into tears at any moment. So Sarah took pity on him.

'But I'm sure if we had a little bit of help as to what we should be looking for in the music we could manage okay?' Sarah nudged her friend in the ribs and pointed to Sivle and shrugged her shoulders. Emma immediately got the point that they couldn't really refuse. Sivle looked like a nervous wreck that could break at any moment.

'Yes we'll need a bit of advice from someone with knowledge but I suppose we should be contributing to the day,' Emma chimed in.

'After all taking part is half the fun right?' she smiled at Sivle who almost burst into tears of gratitude.

'Look we really need to get you two in place before other start showing up because it'll get busy really fast and we just can't have you standing on people by mistake,' said Vanda butting in.

'If you'll just follow me the rest of the introductions will have to wait I'm afraid. We're running out of time.'

Vanda flew across the quarry to the back wall close to the climbing wall and helped settle the girls into their seats.

Someone had gone to a lot of effort trying to make two large old quarry blocks into comfortable seats. There were big cushions everywhere in red, orange, yellow and green and somehow human-sized cups full of juice were laid out on a tray complete with star shaped ice cubes floating in them. There was also a small dish containing what must be fairy floss.

'I thought you ladies would care to try a local delicacy of ours so I arranged some fairy floss for you. It's a thank you for coming along today.' Sivle said this as he arrived behind them somewhat out of breath and sweating a lot even though it was still a cool day and the girls were both wearing jumpers under their jackets.

'Vanda tells me that you humans have something similar called candy floss that's made in big metal drums which sounds too awful. Anyway you must try it.'

'That's very kind of you Sivle,' said Emma picking up the dish and offering it to Emma.

'What a lovely thought. I have to say it looks just like ours. It's even the same shade of pink.'

The girls both picked out a small piece of the fairy floss and, hoping it did taste like the candy floss they were used to, popped it in their mouths. Sarah and Emma both sagged with relief to find it just tasted of sugar and that it dissolved just like candy floss and left them with the same feeling of not being sure if they really wanted to eat more of it or not.

'Well it tastes almost the same as ours. Maybe a little less sweet but it's very nearly identical. Thanks for letting us try Sivle,' said Emma.

Sarah now noticed that other fairies were starting to arrive. There was a steady stream of them entering the old quarry at the same place they had. They came alone, in groups, in teams even – there seemed to be some co-ordination of outfits going on – and there even seemed to be smaller fairies accompanied by larger, presumably older, ones. She asked Sivle if those groups were maybe a school party.

'Indeed they are very well spotted Sarah! Yes we all go to school till we're thirty nine years of age and then after that most of us are done with study. It's only a few like Saphia that carry on. Really our time at school allows us to find out what we're good at, by that age most people have a pretty good idea, and then the teachers just help you learn how to use your particular gift,' replied Sivle.

'You mean if you're good at art but hopeless at science you don't have to do science?' Sarah asked.

'Well of course not!' Sivle replied. 'What would be the point? There's no reason to study something that someone else is clearly better at when you have skills of your own to learn about and improve on. That would be a complete waste of time. I realise we live longer than you but a couple of hundred years isn't really that long at all to perfect a talent. Why waste it on something you won't use once you're forty we say. Now if you'll excuse me for a moment ladies I will be back as soon as I can.'

He turned back momentarily remembering something, 'Thank you again for helping with the piping competition. It is huge relief to me I must say.'

Off Sivle went in the direction of the entrance to the quarry leaving Emma and Sarah alone for the moment to watch the fairies arriving

'What do you make of that?' Sarah asked her friend. 'You only study what you're already good at that way you get really good at it! Imagine that. If you were hopeless at history you don't need to do it.'

'Yes. They certainly have a way of doing things that makes sense to me,' replied Emma.

The girls continued to watch the stream, which was becoming more of a flood, of fairies entering the quarry. They found that they were being stared at just as much as they we're staring themselves.

Vanda had been very clever choosing to seat the girls where she had. All the groups, parties, teams and schools were coming towards the back of the quarry and taking up places in the seats that were everywhere along the back wall. This meant they had to fly, or walk occasionally, past the girls on their heavily padded rocks to get there. Emma and Sarah felt rather like an exhibit in a museum, or like a dummy in a shop front window that gets stared at all day by passers-by. At first they tried to pretend they weren't noticing the attention they were getting but that just became too hard as more and more fairies entered what they were starting to think of as an arena.

Eventually, they decided to chat to a few because it was getting so awkward. It seemed the best thing to do. After the first few comments along the lines of 'Hello how are you? What are you competing in today? And isn't the weather nice?' The flood gates opened. Everyone wanted to talk to them, or rather everyone wanted to say they'd talked to them. One particularly nosey child went on for some time.

'How old are you?' asked a small boy fairy about three inches tall. He was wearing what seemed to be a school uniform, at least everyone he'd arrived with was wearing the same so this seemed to be a safe guess.

It reminded the girls of old-fashioned school uniforms. He wore a baby pink blazer with matching shorts, a white shirt with a school tie of yellow and pink stripes on a brown background and he had white plimsolls on his feet with white socks. For a hat he had a baby pink felt flat cap. Sarah noticed he had a dark red prefect badge stuck into the lapel of his blazer.

'We're both nearly nine years old actually,' Sarah replied. 'How old are you?'

'I'm thirty one next month. Youngest prefect in the school I may add. My name is Ignis and it's a pleasure to meet you,' he replied as he gently lifted up off the floor with delicate wings and hovered in front of the girls at eye level and well above his peers clearly relishing this first contact with a human and how important it would make him appear.

'My name is Sarah and this is my friend Emma,' said Sarah before she asked. 'Is it true that you only study what you're good at in school?'

'Absolutely. There's little point trying to get good at things other people are already gifted at! Take myself for instance, I am a rather exceptional example I have to say, and I specialise in fire. Now that may not sound like much but I'm taking it in a different direction to everyone else. I'm resolved to invent something new. Fire lights and bangs. It's a new thing myself and Saltyp down there have come up with recently and I think it's going to catch on,' said Ignis indicating another boy-fairy in a flat cap some distance below him in the same school group that were now milling around waiting for their friend who was shamelessly talking to the humans. Some were definitely nervous about being this close to the girls. They could see them just itching to move away.

'I'm not sure we know what fire lights and bangs are. Would you mind telling us?' asked Emma.

29

'Ah ha! Just you wait till the end of the games and then you'll see. We managed to persuade the organising committee to let us put a show on at the end. It's going to be the best bit of the whole day I absolutely guarantee it. Anyway what are you doing here?' he asked.

'We've been asked to help with the climbing contest and I think we are judging the piping too,' replied Emma.

'The piping! Wow! That's one tough gig. Just so you know Big Blue hates it if he loses,' Ignis was interrupted by an increased noise level from his classmates below. They wanted to find their seats and he was holding them all up.

'Better dash. They can't do anything without me you know,' and he returned to his classmates and continued on his way.

The flagging and bunting around the back wall of the quarry was starting to make more sense. Teams and schools were assembling in areas where flags were the same colour and design as their uniforms and outfits. Fairies that were arriving as individuals were heading to a different part of the arena where rainbow flags and bunting indicated that anyone could sit there rather than a particular group. The place was really filling up and finally the flow into the quarry was slowing down. The noise level was increasing as people took their seats and chatted to their neighbours. Sarah and Emma also noted that there was a lot of pointing in their direction and they both wished that things would get started so that the attention wouldn't all be on them. It felt so awkward.

'This must be what it's like for an elephant in a room full of meerkats,' said Emma. 'You know you're the biggest but you can't help wishing that they'd stopped bobbing up and down and looking at you all the time.'

They didn't have much longer to suffer the attentions of the fairies though. Vanda was making her way out into the centre of the quarry and onto a small stage that had been set up in the middle. In fact the whole area looked a lot more organised now than when the girls had arrived. It seemed a lot had been done very quickly. Vanda drifted up above the stage slightly and spun slowly looking at the assembled crowd. This made no impression on the background noise level at all so she resorted to shouting.

'CAN I HAVE EVERYONE'S ATTENTION!'

'Wow I didn't know she could be so loud,' whispered Sarah to Emma.

Slowly the noise level subsided and Vanda only needed to repeat herself once more before she got the desired result.

'CAN I HAVE EVERYONE'S ATTENTION! THANK YOU! I would like to welcome you all to the six hundred and forty sixth Highland Games! We have a very busy program of events today including all the old favourites plus a new event specially designed for today. I would like to take a moment to welcome our guest judges Sarah and Emma who are here today to judge the rock climbing and piping events. Can I ask you all to make them most welcome.'

There was a round of applause and a lot of cheering from the assembled fairies. Both Sarah and Emma found themselves blushing bright red but they also felt the need to respond by waving at the assembled fairies being careful not to knock off the ones seated close to their arms on the quarry wall.

'Let us begin, as we traditionally do, with the Four Door Dash. This is a test of speed and agility for our fastest and fittest. Can all the competitors for this event please assemble immediately beside me.'

Vanda's voice was quieter now but it still filled the space well.

A group of around twenty fairies quickly made their way down from the teams and schools areas as well as a few from the individuals seating area. While this happened other fairies were manoeuvring and positioning some fairy sized doors about half a meter above the ground. There were ten rows of four doors, each of the four in one lane was equally spaced from each other, and all the doors were closed. It was a bit like looking at an athletics tracks with its eight lanes set up for the hurdles only instead of hurdles there were doors. At one end Saphia and some others waited to record the times. In the meantime the competitors had self-organised their heats and had arranged themselves into two rows of ten in front of the first line of doors.

'Two heats only today but the fastest ten will proceed to the final. Good luck to you all,' declared Vanda.

Another officially outfitted fairy took control now and set off the first heat of ten. Sarah and Emma watched on in fascination as the first ten fliers set off. It was all quite simple. They flew to the first door, opened it and flew on to the next door opening it and carrying on the same behaviour with all four doors. It was then a short distance to the finish line where a team recorded the times of each flyer across the line. In the meantime the same fairies who had positioned the doors re-closed them ready for the next heat. There was no break at all between the two heats and just as the last flier from the first heat had finished the second heat set off. It seemed that the fairies did everything quickly.

'I wonder how they came up with that race?' Sarah asked no one in particular but loud enough for a few of the fairies near her to hear.

'Oh that's an old one my dear,' said an older fairy to the left of her head. Sarah turned to face them.

'Back in the day, when there were more fairies than there are now, we worked sometimes with humans of a more tolerant nature as messengers. If you wanted a message sent somewhere quickly and privately fairies were the most reliable way.'

'Really? Is that true? Did we used to have a closer friendship to fairies than now?' asked Sarah.

The older fairy sighed, 'It's nobody's fault my dear but after a time humans seemed to change and stopped believing in us. It was as if the fairy stories somehow changed us from something real to something unreal. So we retreated and left humans to get on with their lives without us. It had been fun and we learnt things from each other but we've moved on. This race was a race of the fastest messengers that used to work with the humans. We never let it go.'

With that she turned away from Sarah to discuss something with another fairy seated close to her and Sarah left the conversation there.

Did you hear that?' she asked Emma.

'I certainly did and I think it's sad that we've lost the connection with them. Even stranger to think that fairy stories may not be made up. Just think they could be real! It changes the way you think about them that's for sure.' Sarah said.

'Hey have you noticed that while they started the first event they started a bunch of other events immediately after?'

It was true. The space around them was now full of manic activity. It was hard to keep up with everything that was going on. There seemed to be four or five events happening at the same time. And yes, there was caber tossing just like human Highland Games. Sarah and Emma tried hard to keep up with it all. The tug-of-war was very competitive and there was a lot of audience participation with the noise levels rising by the minute as allegiances between teams became obvious. The girls however didn't have long to wait before they were needed themselves.

'Oh good. You're still here. Now I need you two,' Vanda had materialised between the two girls and was flitting back and forth in front of them until she had their full attention.

'We are going to start the climbing contest. Normally we just have someone up on the top platform there,' she said and pointed to a rocky ledge above them that would be at head height when the girls stood up. It was painted in black and white checkers.

'But seeing as how you've come along you can just stand and watch to see which climber gets there first. Only two climbers climb at a time and whoever wins goes through to the next round. Then they climb against one of the others who won in the first round and we go through the whole thing all over again until there are only

two left. Your job is to give the first to the platform this green flag,'
Vanda flourished a small green flag at them

'Then take their harnesses off them and return them to the
bottom. The climbers need to be very fit as the heats can go on for a
while and the last two climbing are only those with the stamina and
endurance to keep going through all the heats. You'll see some do
really well in their first climb but then they'll get knocked out in the
next round as they have used up all their energy getting through the
first heat.'

'Vanda, why do fairies need harnesses for climbing?' asked
Emma.

'Basically they stop them from cheating.' Vanda replied. 'The
harnesses we wear don't help you stay on ropes and safety lines, the
harnesses we wear strap down wings so you can't use them to fly
with. You can only use your arms and legs just like humans do. It's
a test of strength and stamina.'

'That makes sense. When do we start?' Emma asked.

'Now, here are the first contestants already.' Vanda replied.

The girls turned and looked down to see two fairies wearing
complicated harnesses that held their wings in place coming up to
them. They clipped a small carabineer onto a safety line and, on the
word of another official in a boater hat that had suddenly appeared
they were off and climbing.

Sarah and Emma watched on in amazement, it looked like the
fairies were actually flying, but they couldn't be because their wings
were strapped down. The small bodies of the fairies had less work
to do against gravity as they climbed. The smooth, supple way they
ascended the rock wall reminded Sarah of watching spiders, ants or
little lizards working their way up a wall or window. The stunning
speed they moved at, one on the left and one on the right, meant the
girls had to stand to watch their rapid progress very soon after the
permission to climb was given. One climber started tiring around
waist height to Emma and it was then that the climber opposite
began to really pull away from their competition. This climber kept

up the same pace, with the same level of focus. It was barely a minute from when they started to when they finished and the first climber was already out of the harness and collecting the green flag from Sarah before the other reached the top.

'That was absolutely amazing,' said Sarah as she handed over the flag. 'You must be one of the favourites to win today.'

'Oh no,' replied the fairy. 'That would be my sister. Just you wait till she climbs. It's like watching water flowing down a stream only up a wall instead. She's my hero.'

With that comment he took off from the ledge back to the floor receiving polite applause from the seats nearest the climbing wall.

Emma and Sarah were kept very busy returning harnesses to the bottom of the wall and watching the progress of the climbers. They lost track of all the other events that were going on. Sarah thought she recognised the fairy that 'climbed like flowing water' in one of the heats. She stood out from all the rest because she climbed so effortlessly and elegantly. Her opponent had applauded - from somewhere around knee height - as she had reached the top. Sarah also reckoned she could recognise at least one other climber who could make it into the final against her but there were more heats to come.

Spending time with the fairies and finally doing a job, rather than just being a spectacle to be looked at, meant the girls started to relax and enjoy themselves more. They chatted with the competitors congratulating those that won and being encouraging to those that lost. Some of the fairies seated closest to the climbing wall were relaxing too and began to sharing information with the two girls about whom the competitors were and who they thought likely to win. It seemed that the fairies quite lost their sense of reserve around the girls now that they had the shared common ground of the competition to talk about.

It must have been a good half an hour of heats before the final round. The sister of the young fairy Sarah had talked to was indeed taking part. She and her competitor were chatting at the base of the rock wall and resting before their final pitch of the day. They were two very different fairies. The 'waterfall fairy', as Sarah had come to think of her, was only four inches tall and lithe of limb. She was slender and petite and seemed very unassuming and unconcerned by the attention she was getting from the seats either side of the climbing wall. The fairies watching on the wall had decided who was their favourite as the competition progressed and now it seemed as though the support for the two final climbers was equally matched. Her competition couldn't have been more different. He stood at easily seven inches in height and was all muscle. He looked twice the size of his opposition and was waving enthusiastically to his supporters in the crowd around him clearly revelling in the attention he was getting.

'And climb!' The official at the base of the wall announced the beginning of the event with no introduction and it took the crowd by surprise. The two climbers though had been ready and were both off quickly up the lower section of the wall. By now they had both climbed six times that morning and Sarah expected to see them move a little slower than before but that didn't seem to be the case. Unassuming as the 'waterfall fairy' clearly was she certainly wanted to win and was in the lead from very early on. There were a few moments when it looked like the strength of the other climber would mean she would be caught but determination was etched on her face throughout and she reached the platform moments ahead of her rival. She just had time to reach down to help him up over the final ledge and then the two of them embraced and smiled warmly at each other.

A huge cheer went up from the crowd. It was a popular result and Sarah said to Emma that she thought it was very sportsman like that they had hugged at the end of the race. She was overheard through the noise by the small fairy who she had first spoken to at the end of the first heat and he let her in on the secret.

'That's my dad and my sister. He taught her everything she knows and this is the first time she's beaten him and it was in front of everyone here today too. Wow!' and without waiting for her to reply he joined his sister and father on the platform and the three celebrated together.

'That's kind of cool,' said Emma to Sarah, 'they're a talented climbing family that's for sure. They are so supportive of each other. Just look at them.'

But the girls had no time to watch or talk to the fairies that had just climbed. Oh no, because here again came Vanda.

'Sarah and Emma thank you so much for helping out but now I think we need to start the piping. Most of the track and field events are over and we've already started the dancing over there,' she indicated a raised platform where dancers seemed to be doing a jig of some kind that involved a ball and bits of ribbon. It didn't make a lot of sense to the girls.

'You are now needed back down at ground level please. Where that other platform is? Off to the right there? Well that's your next job. Sivle will meet you there to assist in the judging. The competitors know he is not judging only assisting in technical matters. Off you go now and good luck.' Vanda didn't wait for them to ask any questions she just vanished again.

'I'm sure she's avoiding telling us exactly how hard this is.' Emma said.

'You think?' said Sarah, 'I know she is.'

The girls, concentrating hard on where they were placing their feet so as not to stand on any equipment lying around, or unsuspecting fairies, made their way over to the platform indicated by Vanda.

Here they found a small group of fairies, maybe only a dozen, waiting along with Sivle. Sivle looked nervous and was sweating a lot having to pat his forehead dry constantly with a handkerchief he kept producing from his pocket. It wasn't surprising he looked nervous. These were by far the biggest fairies the girls had seen all day. Some of them looked closed to nine inches tall, maybe even ten. They were all big, they all had huge muscles and when they flexed their arms it was like each muscle was fighting to look bigger than the others. Most striking was the huge barrel chests they had, they literally looked like barrels round the middle. They all had very serious expressions too. This wasn't light musical entertainment, this was musical war.

Clearly playing the pipes was not for the faint hearted and for the first time the girls imagined how music could be a competitive sport without having heard a note played yet.

Sivle looked a little more comfortable, and a lot more relieved, when Sarah and Emma arrived.

'Ah lovely ladies and honoured judges! I am so very glad to see you have joined us for this most prestigious of events. I have arranged for one of the pipers to give you a demonstration before we start the competition proper so I can appraise you on some of the finer points of this most noble of instruments.'

One of the tall, muscled pipers stepped forward from the group and towered over Sivle. He wore, as they all did, a tartan kilt and matching sash round the body. Apart from that they wore nothing, no shoes or hat or shirt. This piper's tartan was red and purple check with flashes of yellow. In front of the platform on which they would perform were tables set out holding the pipes. These were in groups of three pipes made from different rocks, some were grey and others pink, and each pipe was separately made but bound to two others with strong looking twine. The pipes were of different length and widths with the shorter thinner ones being strapped together and likewise the fatter longer ones. With no announcement at all the piper picked up a short thin selection of pipes and started blowing softly down one end of the pipes moving his mouth across the top of the pipes much like the human version of a pan pipe. The noise though was so high pitched the girls could barely make out the notes at all. Suddenly, the piper reached out to grab the next pipe group on the table which were longer and a little wider. While the girls could still hear the notes from the other pipe dying away he began piping on the new set. The notes were in a slightly lower register and Sarah and Emma could now make out the tune clearly rather than it being on the edge of hearing. The piper continued to switch out the pipes he was using, the deeper notes from the longer and wider pipes demanded more attention when playing as well as breath. The piper's face turned quite scarlet when working through the notes these pipes played as so much puff was required to get the low notes that they thought the poor fairy was close to passing out and it was hard to enjoy the music because of their concern for the musician. All the while Sivle spoke in a low voice to them about the skill of playing the pipes so as not to interrupt.

'You can see that considerable skill and strength and speed is required to play the pipes. Technical difficulty counts for a lot and is considered in two ways. One is in the difficulty of swopping a lot between different pipe sets, there are twelve in all, and a piece of music with more than twenty transitions between pipes is considered quite hard. The other technical difficulty relates to those played all in the lower register, those deep notes as you can see are difficult to achieve and put the piper in a state of physical distress after a short period of time. Pieces that involve more than a third of their playing on the bass parts are also considered technically more demanding and will afford additional points. Regarding the execution of the music itself I think you may need to defer to my knowledge, you have never heard these works before and have no knowledge of what a good rendition sounds like. However in terms of judging the technical nature of a piece I think you will master it quite quickly. Please note that on occasion a piper will pass out attempting a piece that they aren't quite ready for yet and that is an instant disqualification from the event. You must start and finish a piece, there are no allowances given to those who do not.'

Sarah and Emma listened to his words while also listening to the piper. The music was quite haunting really, it sounded like the wind moving through the trees or blowing through grass, and it was in fact rather relaxing. It reminded Emma of the music her Aunt played when she was practicing yoga in the house. The piper that had volunteered to play for the girls finished his piece and stepped back into the crowd of the other pipers. They didn't applaud his efforts but he did receive nods of approval and a touch on the arm from one or two which seemed to be all he was going to get.

The other games around the quarry were finishing up now and the atmosphere was definitely changing. What had a few minutes ago been a place of wild cheering and encouragement was turning into one of quiet attentiveness. The seats were all full, many of the competitors from the earlier events had re-joined their friends, and there was a building air of expectation. The focus of attention was now the platform by which the girls stood and finally they appreciated the seriousness of the role they had agreed to play. A few of the organising committee and officials were moving more pipe sets up onto the stage and the first piper joined them.

'You should know that not all the pieces you will hear will be like the one you have just heard.' Sivle said quietly to the girls.

'We have music to dance to, music to laugh to, music to cry to, music for war and music of love. We have no rules as to what the pipers play but you will see that the most skilled will bring all those watching on a journey through the music. You will know who has won outright because the real judges are sitting around you. You may choose the most technically proficient piece as the winner but it may be another that has captured the minds and the hearts of the audience.'

The girls were increasingly alarmed as to the extent of the task they were taking on but realised there was no way they could back out.

A hush fell over the quarry and all ears bent in the direction of the pipers. There was no announcement that the competition would begin, it wasn't necessary, everyone knew. The first piper selected a set of pipes, took a deep breath, bowed to the other contestants and the judges and began.

What happened in the next hour or so was something the girls would never forget. They later would both tell each other that they

40

could never describe it to anyone but they considered themselves incredibly lucky to have been there and to have heard the things they did that morning in the quarry at the back of the Fawcett's Farm.

No piper chose the same piece as any other. It was obvious early on that the younger, less practiced pipers were taking to the stage first. It was accepted that the older fairies would play later but even so the sounds the younger fairies produced would certainly be described as magical by Sarah or Emma. Notes that came from the pipes could sound like drums as well as wind, they could even sound like brass instruments such as the trumpet or French horn and there was even a piper who made the rock pipes sing like a flute.

While the girls struggled to concentrate on the technical aspects of what they were hearing they found it hard to concentrate. Some of the tunes made them want to dance, they were full of joy and hope and happiness and in parts of the quarry little groups of fairies did indeed dance along to the tunes. Others made them think of the saddest thing they had ever felt in their lives and they, along with the attentive audience, shed silent tears as the high strains of the smallest pipes floated above them in the still air.

Between each rendition Sarah, Emma and Sivle judged the performances on technical and artistic merit but it became harder and harder to separate the performances as the older pipers took to the stage. Their proficiency with the pipes seemed to be equal and the only difference was in the choice of music and the response that their choice was eliciting from the audience. When the final piper stepped up onto the stage the tension built still further.

Big Blue, the piper Sivle seemed the most nervous of and who was wearing a blue kilt, had just played an uplifting piece that had made Sarah think of all her favourite people together being happy and enjoying each others' company. She felt fabulously light and giggly at the end of it and thought it had been brilliant. The look on Emma's face told her that she had also been impressed.

The last piper waited a moment for the crowd to settle before beginning. He chose differently, he chose music that took their

41

minds out of the quarry and let them float over the hills, flying over the countryside and letting them see how amazing the land beneath them was. It was a hauntingly beautiful tune that created a feeling of connectedness, like they were all part of the same creature living in the same space, striving for the same things in harmony. It was a tune that spoke of love, but not love for family and friends, love of everything.

'It makes you so happy just to be alive doesn't it?' said Emma quietly when he finished.

Sarah just nodded in reply. It felt like that music had found a place to sit inside her and it was never going to go away. It felt magical.

'I think we've found the winner for today,' she said quietly to Emma and Sivle.

All around the stadium fairies were slowly rising up from their seats as a chorus of approval met the last performance that began as a small scattering of applause that grew in volume as others joined in. The fairies were not simply applauding a good performance they were thanking the piper for what he had just given them. No announcement was required. Everyone, including Big Blue, knew who had won and he was the first to join the winner on the stage and raise his hand to show he was the better piper on the day. It was then the cheering grew even louder with laughter also. Big Blue's fearsome reputation was seemingly not going to be so fearsome from now on.

Ignis, the small fairy Sarah had spoken to at the start of the day appeared by her shoulder.

'Now get a load of this!' he exclaimed as he continued flying past her and back towards the rock climbing wall.

An eruption of lights drew everyone's attention. Somehow, the sky had grown dark, or maybe the invisible ceiling they had had been turned to dim but brilliant points and splashes of light were appearing to light up the sky. They were brilliant and vibrant and dazzling. Some of the younger fairies began crying in fright

42

needing comforting from the older ones. There were flashes of colours brilliant like falling autumn leaves, and others bright like diamonds sparking in the sun. Some flowed together mixing reds and oranges like a great sunset that dimmed quickly to be replaced by turquoise and yellow of a tropical beach. There were loud bangs too that accompanied bursts of white light like dandelion seed heads exploding. It didn't last long but it was very impressive. The fairies applauded at the end and Ignis and his friend Saltyp bowed from a rock ledge they were perched on that was being highlighted by two waterfalls of white light on either side.

The pair seemed very pleased with their efforts even though no one seemed to have actually noticed them up there.

'Thank you all for coming along to the Highland Games today everyone.' Vanda had flown to the middle of the quarry and was making another announcement.

'For all those here the presentations will happen later in the Great Hall and will be accompanied by refreshments. Thanks to Ignis and Saltyp for their fire lights and bangs display just now. Clearly we have some real talent amongst our younger fairies and I'm sure we will have more fire lights and bangs in the future. Thanks also to our superb guest judges Sarah and Emma for their assistance today.'

A polite ripple of applause filled the space and Sarah and Emma went right back to feeling embarrassed again although they waved at the crowds of fairies anyway.

With that the quarry started to empty. There was a fair amount of noise as people swopped stories from the day or congratulated each other on their performances. Vanda, Tattle and Saphia made their way over to Sarah and Emma who were too afraid to move with the sheer mass of fairies surrounding them. They didn't want to accidentally crush one of them and cause some kind of incident after such a successful day. However, with the appearance of the three fairies they suddenly remembered that their real job that day hadn't been to judge piping and climbing.

There really is a problem

'So now you have seen what's really going on,' said Vanda taking off her boater hat and letting her hair fall free.

'It may have not been so obvious to you but there were many competitors who pulled out of the events today, either before or during, as they simply weren't fit enough. The doctors we had on standby have had a busy morning too. Hippy, you remember Hippy don't you? He treated Del's broken wing?'

The girls nodded as they thought back, not that very long ago to when they'd met a fairy who'd been turned into a duck.

'Well Hippy says that most of the time they have nothing to do at these events. Today we had strained muscles, exhaustion, and even a suspected heart attack. The poor man is going to be fine but he'll need to go on a diet and take things easy for a couple of days. He was in the middle of tossing a caber when it happened and it landed on his foot. The broken toe was easy to fix but mending hearts isn't something we can do. Hippy is worried. Until today he hadn't realised how unfit people had become and how many of them had gained weight. I think it's because it's all happened so fast. He wants to help if he can and I think there are others who have quietly noticed too and are concerned but aren't saying anything yet.'

Saphia interrupted Vanda. She could see that if they started discussing this now it could be difficult to stop.

'Look we really don't have time to do this right now as we have to get back and do all the presentations. If we can delay the talking until tomorrow that would be for the best. It'll give all of us a chance to sleep on what we've seen today and consider our course of action. I think Hippy may want to be more involved too.'
'Agreed,' said Emma, 'I've seen more than I bargained for today and need some time to think things through.'

That seemed to be the end of the matter and the girls and fairies parted ways. Sarah and Emma made sure that their return to the

Fawcett's Farm came from a completely different direction than the quarry and they spent the rest of the day together talking through everything they'd seen and done.

'I'm glad that I have someone to share all this with.' Emma said, 'Imagine if you had these fairy friends all to yourself and no one to share this with? I'm not sure I could cope keeping it all to myself.'

'Well imagine what it was like for me before you got involved. I wasn't sure if I was going mad or not. I was pretty sure I wasn't but when you have no one else who knows it certainly makes you feel pretty alone.' Sarah replied.

'Anyway, back to what we should be thinking about. Did you notice the general fitness and size of the fairies? Did you think they looked any different to normal?'

'Well now I've had a bit of time to think I'd have to say yes. I mean Sivle looked terrible and that wasn't just because he was scared of the big piper either! The school kids didn't look so bad to me.'

Emma stopped walking and folded her arms in front of her while she gave it some serious consideration. 'I was trying to pay attention to the tug-o-war and the caber tossing. Now I think about it the earlier heats in both of those events went very quickly. Some of the tug-of-war teams seemed barely capable of picking up the rope never mind pulling over the team on the other end of it. They went out of the competition very quickly. It's the same with the caber tossing. They started out on small timbers, there weren't that many that made it through the early rounds onto the bigger ones. I don't know if that's normal but knowing how competitive the fairies are I can't imagine they entered just for fun. They all enter to win regardless of what they say to each other. I am wondering now if some of those that got knocked out in the earlier rounds were surprised at how quickly they were removed from the competition. It would be good to talk to Hippy and find out what the injuries were and what the patients were saying.'

'Well let's hope he comes along tomorrow.' Sarah said.

The girls spent a great afternoon outdoors in the brilliant weather that doesn't happen often in the Lake District but makes it all the more beautiful when it does. They thought the place looked especially lovely and realised it was partly caused by the music the last piper has chosen to play. Eventually, they parted ways knowing that tomorrow they would meet with the 'Free Fairies From Floss' team, as they had now dubbed the group of ladies, and find out more.

After breakfast the next day Emma walked down the lane to Sarah's Aunt Jane's cottage to collect her. They took Bertie, the collie dog with them out into another day of beautiful sunshine.

'Now enjoy the weather while it lasts girls. You know it won't be around for long!'

That had been Aunt Jane's parting words for them after she'd made sure Sarah was carrying a waterproof jacket in her bag 'just in case' as she put it. They headed towards one of the smaller streams at the base of the hill away from the cottage and farm. They planned to walk along this little beck and see what they could find keeping an eye out for herons who sometimes fished on the bank. Sarah was anxious to meet up with the fairies and was rubbing the small crystal Vanda had given her in her pocket. It had the desired effect as it wasn't long before Vanda, along with Saphia, Tattle and Hippy, appeared

'Oh good. We were starting to wonder if you'd ever call today,' said Vanda accusingly who was looking quite put out.

'We didn't know you were waiting on us to contact you!' exclaimed Sarah.

'Well we're all here now and that's what matters,' said Saphia stepping in before it became an issue.

'We need to get down to business. I propose we allow Hippy to tell us first what he thought of yesterday. He knows the most about the general health of our clan and I suspect his information will help guide how we decide to proceed in this matter.'

The others all agreed that this seemed like a sensible thing to do.

'Thank you Saphia. And allow me to express my delight at seeing these two lovely young ladies again. It would seem you are becoming invaluable to our little community and I believe that I am glad of it. To begin I would like to say that patient confidentiality is paramount. I shall name no names so please do not ask me to. I shall refer in general terms to what I have observed now that I have had my eyes opened to the issue at hand.'

Hippy settled on a lower branch of a silver birch tree and looked like he was going to take some time speaking. The others also got comfortable in the surrounding undergrowth while the girls found large rounded rocks to sit on. It felt like they were waiting for the teacher to begin class.

'I am shocked and saddened by what I have seen. It is clear that a vast change has come over quite a large number of us. I would estimate at around fifty percent. The change I refer to is a gaining of a considerable amount of weight, again it is an estimate, but I think around a twenty percent increase in many and up to thirty five to forty percent in the worst cases.'

He sighed deeply before carrying on and it was quite clear that he was upset by what he'd seen.

'This apparent weight gain will be placing a massive stress on the internal organs and joints of the fairies. Yesterday we saw minor injuries such as small tears in muscles as well as more serious injuries where dislocations of joints required treating. At least ten competitors reported considerable shortness of breath, the nature of which was serious enough to require medical treatment, and there was one gentleman who's heart had undergone such stress it briefly ceased to work. Luckily we managed to revive him but it was a nasty turn that he may never fully recover from.'

'Let me say that we have the skills to treat all of these problems however we have never had to in the past. Not at a Highland Games event and never in such numbers. The nature of these injuries and the sheer number of them caught us quite off guard. Those of us in the medical tent quickly realised that we had a considerable problem and started collating data on the patients and their concerned friends and relatives as soon as we could hence I have some degree of confidence in the numbers I give you today. It is truly a problem and I am inclined to believe Vanda when she claims that the cause of all this misery is the increased consumption of fairy floss in recent times. It would appear to be the only significant change to have taken place in the diets and behaviour of the fairies recently. Whatever we are looking at is certainly not something that has crept up slowly. It has erupted as quickly as a beehive would if attacked and we must do all in our power to stop it and quickly.'

Hippy was looking genuinely distressed by what he was saying.

'Should this weight gain continue at the rapid rate it has begun we won't just have a few torn muscles and some out of breath fairies, we will have fatalities. I realise this sounds dramatic but I think it is true. Our bodies cannot cope for long with such a massive increase in weight as the stress on internal organs and their functions will be simply overwhelming. It greatly saddens me that this is happening and the cause seems to be the fairies themselves.'

He took a breath to calm down and looked at the others, 'I am not one to interfere in the lives of others but I have a duty of care to my patients. I care deeply about these people and I will not allow them to eat themselves to death without trying to do something to stop it!' He sat down, looking grimly determined and waited for one of the others to continue where he'd left off.

They were all a little bit reticent to say anything instead allowing what he'd said to really sunk in. It was a moment or two before Saphia spoke up.

'Well I'm not sure I can add much after that. The results from yesterday's games show that, for competitors who had taken part previously, there was a considerable reduction in the times taken, or weight lifted, or distance thrown or whatever you wish to judge them against. Our fairies are slower and weaker than they were ten years ago.' She turned specifically to Sarah and Emma to explain.

48

'Humans don't know it but fairies only really get weak just as they are losing their powers before they die. Once we are adults our abilities remain relatively constant for several hundred years except in exceptional circumstances. The differences in the performances should have been much smaller than we observed. Some of the runners were twenty percent slower and they knew it. As a timing referee for the day I could see the shock and distress on the finishing line when they realised how much slower they were. The same applies to other events. I think the Games demonstrated to them exactly how much they had changed. This may shock some of them into taking action. Others may just put it down to having a bad day and ignore that there is really an issue. Only time will tell.'

Having said her piece Saphia sat down on the branch she was occupying and closed the file she had been reading from.

'Well I for one am desperately disappointed by yesterday!' Tattle, the vivacious, bubbly, smiley Tattle looked utterly defeated and tired. Her hair was drawn back in a tight pony tail that accentuated the obvious fact that she had hardly slept at all that night. She had on a baggy track suit that almost enveloped her in a mass of fabric. It was so big it looked like a sleeping bag.

'I cannot believe that my fellow fairies have let this happen to themselves. As a trainer and fitness professional it is heartbreaking to see what I saw yesterday not to mention that no one took part in my new Racing Round event!'

'That was probably for the best my dear.' Hippy said, 'if they had, given its difficulty as you described it to me, I feel certain we could have had a fatality on the field. But don't be too hard on yourself. It is not your fault this has happened.' Hippy flew over to her and put a comforting arm around her shoulders.

'So this is it,' said Vanda sternly. 'We are agreed that we have to do something. We are agreed that the most likely cause is the massive overeating of fairy floss and we are agreed that we need to act now? Raise your hand if you are in agreement.'

The little group looked to each other as each of them in turn nodded and raised their hand in agreement with Vanda. The time had come to stop talking and to take action.

'So what do you propose we do?' asked Hippy.

'Obviously I have been giving this a considerable amount of thought,' replied Vanda.

She now took up a position in the centre of the group. 'Firstly I believe we need to find whoever is responsible for this, we suspect it is a fairy named Gula so we need to find out why she is doing this and see if she can be stopped through reasoning with her.'

'However, I doubt that will be the case and so I believe we also need to find where she is keeping the spiders to supply all this fairy floss and release them in the more likely case of her refusing to do so voluntarily. If the supply dries up people will no longer be tempted by it. I cannot accept that the spiders should be supplying floss for so long. It isn't right. I propose that Saphie and I take on that role.'

Vanda turned to the dishevelled Tattle, 'Tattle I need you to pull yourself together. I need you out there providing free classes and getting the fairies back in the gym or exercising more. I don't care how you do it and I don't care who else you get involved just do what you do best. If you really care then you can do something about it and that means starting right now.'

Now she turned her focus onto the good doctor, 'In the meantime if Hippy can get the other doctors to start making some house calls and encouraging those in greatest need of change to stop eating this stuff that could be very helpful too. Our fairies may be addicted to this stuff, or it may be enchanted for all we know, but they need your help either way.'

Finally she turned her attention to the girls, 'Sarah and Emma I don't know as yet what role there is for you in all this but I am sure there will be. I hope you will be available to us should the need arise and we will keep you informed as to our progress.'

'It would appear you have given this considerable thought,' said Hippy. 'I shall certainly hold up my end of the deal and I will use the assistance of my medical colleagues. Together we will try. With that in mind if you ladies would excuse me we have a lot to do.'

Hippy bowed to them and promptly vanished.

'I'm not sure I'll ever get completely used to fairies just popping in and out like that,' said Sarah. 'Because I never know when it's going to happen it means I'm nervous the whole time. I suppose we will just wait and see if you need us,' she said to Vanda.

'Well I don't think you'll have to wait too long. I have a meeting set up with this Gula person in half an hour,' said Saphia. 'I intend to get to the bottom of all this before the day is done. I would think that you will hear from us again quite soon Sarah.'

'I can't stand this,' burst out Tattle. 'I have to do something about it! I hate being miserable and I will not tolerate this anymore. I'm off to get some fairies training!'

She also vanished followed by Saphia and Vanda leaving the girls quite alone again.

Gula

Vanda and Saphia stood in a room that was too small for its contents. It was an office that was also a library that was also a wardrobe. Somehow they managed to fit themselves in between the piles of books, files, clothes and bric-a-brac that threatened to break down the walls and spill out of the door. They had to be careful not to knock anything over. The woman they had come to see was standing next to a desk and she did not look happy. She was easily six inches tall and had the longest, blackest hair they'd seen. It was woven throughout with fine thread on which tiny pearls and silver stars had been placed. Her hair was matched by her equally dramatic dress of deepest burgundy red that was highlighted here and there by the same silver stars and tiny pearls. Nothing about her bearing said 'how nice to see you we're going to be such good friends'.

'Ladies. To what do I owe this uncalled for visit? I am sorry but I only have a few minutes to spare today I am quite busy.' She seated herself at the desk, placed a small pair of spectacles on her nose, and made a show of looking over some papers.

Vanda and Saphia glanced at each other. Who would go first? It looked like Vanda.

'Well if you have no time for visitors then I will speak plainly,' said Vanda folding her arms across her chest defensively. 'I want to know if you are the one who has been selling the fairy floss and buying all the pages up in the Fabulous Fairy.'

She jutted her chin out and looked hard at the fairy called Gula in front of her as if daring her to deny it.

'Well of course I am! You came all the way to see me to ask me that! Is that all? Yes my business is doing very nicely thank you for asking. I do hope you have sampled it yourself?' Gula replied throwing her arms open wide to accept the accusation as if it were a compliment.

Vanda was unmoved, 'I presume you know the damage you are doing to people? Are you aware of the terrible state of health your product is getting fairies into?' Vanda threw the questions back like knives.

'Oh come now. Be reasonable,' said Gula calmly as she rose from her seat, 'I have done nothing to them.'

'That's a lie!' retorted Vanda, 'There are fairies with health problems we have never seen before and it's your fault! You cannot say the responsibility is not yours!'

'You misunderstand me dear girl,' replied Gula no longer smiling as she approached Vanda.

'I have myself done nothing. I have simply provided them with something they wanted. They have made their own choice to eat it. I did not stand over them and force it down their throats did I?'

Gula was standing right in front of Vanda and she raised her eyebrow and tilted her head to one side looking as innocent as a lamb. 'I think you'll find that they have made their own decision to eat it. I simply supply the market with what they want.'

Vanda was temporarily speechless. She hadn't expected this open confession as a response. Her confusion was obvious and Gula turned to Saphia instead.

'And you? What do you have to say? You must be the faithful side kick. The one who always backs up her friend in her silly petty schemes? Always in the shadows never in the spotlight?'

Saphia looked momentarily stunned, but then rallied, setting her shoulders square and staring Gula straight in the eye.

'Don't presume you understand our friendship. I would not in fact expect someone like you to understand what friendship is. You've clearly never had any friends and if you continue to behave the way you are you never will.'

It was Gula's turn to look perturbed and she took a small step back, you would only have seen if you had been looking for it, and Saphia had been. What Saphia said next however made her lose her composure.

'I came here to assist my friend in finding out if you were the one who was supplying the huge quantities of fairy floss we are seeing in the markets. It would appear that that task was not as hard as we had thought as you have openly admitted it.' Saphia took a slow, considered look around the room they were in before continuing. She had both Vanda and Gula's full attention.

'I came here because I wanted two things. Firstly, I wanted to know what it was like to be banished without good reason with your family when you were only a child who wouldn't have understood what was happening or why. Secondly, I came because I wanted to offer my help in assisting you redress the wrong that was done to you and your parents as I believe it was a terrible misuse of power for which someone should answer. Due to the lack of records on the matter I do not know who that is. However, it would seem that you think you would not need any such help nor appreciate friendship should it be offered. Given your position I see no point in wasting your time or ours anymore and we shall leave. Come on Vanda we are going.'

Saphia took Vanda's arm in her own and strode out through the door that they had come in and did not look back. If she had she would have seen Gula return slowly to the chair and sand into it placing her elbows on the desk and her head in her hands.

'She was quite insufferable,' said Vanda once they were clear of the house. 'But you showed her Saphie. I had no idea you could be so, what's the word I'm looking for, so harsh?'

'I simply decided a long time ago not to suffer fools and she clearly is one. I was not going to spend my time trying to reason with someone who wished to remain such a closed book. I see now she knows well enough what she is about.'

Saphia took her friends hand and walked her over to a seat where they could talk quietly together. 'Having said that we aren't seeing things from her point of view and that's important.'

'What's that supposed to mean Saphie?

'What that means Vanda is we need to imagine what it must be like to have flown a mile in her wings. Put yourself in her place imagine what you've been through to get here and imagine what it would have done to you along the way. Now consider that and tell me what you think.' Saphia waited for her friend to collect her thoughts. It took a few moments while Vanda gave this some consideration and then she spoke carefully.

'I would be angry. I would have been a child when we had to leave and I would not have understood why and my parents wouldn't have told me because they would have been angry and upset too.' Vanda's brow furrowed as she concentrated.

'They wouldn't have been able to tell me why we had to leave because they didn't know why they were banished either. So I would hate the people that did it to us.' She looked at her friend with big wide eyes as the penny dropped. 'I would hate the people who had done it and I would want them to hurt as much as they had hurt us! She's doing this out of revenge isn't she?'

'That is certainly my working hypothesis. I feel a little bit sorry for her. Imagine. Your family is discredited and thrown out. You have no appeal, no way to challenge and years and years later you come back. All that time to think about it, all those days spent planning what you'd do to the people that hurt you. I can imagine that revenge is quite probably all the motivation she needs now to carry on.' Saphia sighed, 'I was speaking truthfully. I did want to offer my help. I thought that such a gesture may be seen in friendship and conciliation but I am not sure that Gula will ever see it that way. She has spent too long by herself nursing the hate and the revenge.'

The two got up and continued their walk in silence.

'What I want to know is why she came back.' Saphia said almost to herself, 'Why would you come back and be here, why not just do all this from a distance? Why come right back to where it must hurt the most to be? And where are her parents? Are they even still alive?' she mused out loud.

'We have bigger problems that that though,' Vanda said quietly.

'We know that she does not intend to stop supplying. Our problem now is we don't know where all the fairy floss is coming from but we need to find out. If Gula won't stop we will have to do it for her or fairies will start dying. We are going to need help finding the spiders Saphie. We need to find those spiders and let them go. If we can do that then she can't keep poisoning our friends with this horrible sugary stuff!'

'You're absolutely right Vanda. We need to follow the fairies making the deliveries and find out where they go. What did you have planned for the afternoon?'

'Oh just a fitting for a new frock, it can wait though. I'm rather enjoying this truthfully. I feel like I'm helping. I feel this is the right thing to do. You know ever since I met Sarah I've been feeling more confident and more sure of myself.'

'I must say I've noticed a change in you too but I like to think it's you just finally growing up!' Saphia said.

Vanda hugged her friend before saying, 'No chance of that Saphie dear! Who'd want to be a grown up? They have no fun at all.'

The fairies took off in the direction of the shops and markets where the biggest supplies of fairy floss could be found.

Saphia's new clothes

Vanda was an accomplished shopper. This gave her skills that Saphia had not fully appreciated until today. As they wove around between shops, carts, people and stalls Vanda negotiated it with the air of a cat sauntering around her personal territory. Wherever she was others were aware of her presence. Some reacted as equals with greetings and pleasantries exchanged. Others tried to entice her into their shop or show her their latest goods. Still others seemed to shrink away from her as if remembering some past unpleasantness. Vanda glided through it all unrushed. She smiled and nodded to some, politely declined the advances of others and completely ignored quite a few too.

Here, thought Saphia, she seems to be a queen. Here Vanda was in her natural habitat and knew everyone and saw everything. Saphia hadn't fully appreciated the thrall Vanda held on the social status and standings of others. She supposed – now that she considered it for the first time – that if Vanda was seen in your dress, or carrying your bag in the Fabulous Fairy, then others would want what she had and the sales at those establishments would go up.

Saphia herself had never really understood why this sort of thing happened but she couldn't deny that it did. Now she was observing the effect this had it was quite remarkable and she couldn't help but comment on it to her friend.

'People here treat you like a hawk, or fox, something to be feared and respected. It's amazing! I've never seen anything like it before!'

'My dearest Saphie. Of course they do! I can make or break sales for some of these people! I set trends and fashions. Where I lead others follow! Well some do anyway.' Vanda replied looking at her friend like she had only just noticed her for the first time that day.

'And some could do with paying more attention it seems. When was the last time you wore something other than black? You do know that's so last decade don't you? We really ought to go shopping together sometime. I could really make you shine.'

Vanda looked pleased at her idea and beamed a lovely smile at her friend before carrying on down the street.

Saphia was momentarily taken aback but rallied well. 'I've always worn black! Its classic! Black never goes out of style! And anyway it suits me!'

'Yes dear it does but it also suits dead people. It doesn't say anything about you as a person other than I couldn't be bothered this morning! Anyway some of your black is so old its grey,' continued Vanda, 'I will come round to yours tomorrow and we'll go through your wardrobe together. No need to thank me but I'll be doing you a favour.'

Vanda, considering the matter done, swept on through the crowded area and Saphia, not wanting to lose her, struggled to keep up as the melee of people simply closed up behind Vanda once she had passed. Saphia was unsettled by this line of conversation.

'Do you really think of me like that?' she asked her friend in a small hurt voice. 'Do you really see me as dull as a dead person?'

Vanda stopped suddenly causing Saphia to bump into her. 'Of course I don't! Why you're the smartest fairy I know and I'm lucky to have you as a friend! I often wonder why you bother to spend time with me you're so much smarter and better at everything than me!'

Vanda hugged her friend warmly and Saphia smiled inside. 'No that's not what I think at all but it is what others will see and what others will think.'

'What do you mean?' Saphia was confused by this.

'Think about it,' sighed Vanda, 'I know you. I've known you all my life. We talk, we share and we are a big part of each other's lives. I see you for what you are because I know you. Others,' and with this she waved her arms around indicating the world in general, 'don't know you. They don't know how brilliant you are, they don't know that you're the best kind of fairy there is. They don't see you for your amazing personality. They just see a fairy all in black that doesn't say much and exudes an air of 'leave me aloneness'. Don't you see? You don't know lots of people and have lots of friends because your appearance has made you unapproachable. Combine that with your tendency not to share much and it makes you a sort of prickly cactus. They don't know what to think about you so they tend to not bother. I'm sorry. It's not how things should be it's just the way people are I'm afraid.'

'I don't mind not having lots of friends. I like the friends I have and I like my own company. I don't need everyone to like me,' retorted Saphia. 'I don't think I want people to like me for what I look like! That's so superficial.'

'It is isn't it,' replied Vanda, 'I know that too and yet it's the truth. When you fly around the flowers don't you look at the colour? Don't you smell the roses in summer? Don't you love seeing the first daffodils and bluebells in spring? On a beautiful sunny day isn't the colour of the sky an amazing blue and the sparkle on the water something that catches your eye?'

'Well of course. Nature is beautiful and those things all make me happy,' replied Saphia. 'I don't know what you're getting at?'

'What I'm getting at dear, smart Saphie, is that yes nature is wonderful and it's bright and colourful and changes with the seasons. We are part of nature too and so we see each other as we see nature. We aren't daffodils or bluebells that only have colour for a few short weeks to then disappear underground for another year. We live all year and we can celebrate the beauty of the changes in the season by changing ourselves. The way I see it is if you wear black all the time you aren't accepting your nature and your colours. You are missing out on expressing who you are. Do you see what I'm trying to say?'

'Maybe,' replied Saphia slowly. 'So because I am in black all the time it's kind of saying keep away? And others don't notice me because we're attracted to colour and changes and something that is dark and unchanging isn't something we're naturally attracted to because in nature we wouldn't be either?'

'You may have over complicated it but definitely something like that,' replied Vanda. 'Look. Once people know you they love you but you make yourself hard to notice because you never catch the eye in the way a daffodil does. I'm saying that people don't notice you.' Vanda hugged her friend again before carrying on through the crowds again.

Saphia fell silent. She needed some time to think about this and whether it was a real thing or something random her friend had just invented. She was happy, she liked the friends she had, she never thought about what other people thought of her or what she looked like. For the first time she considered if this meant she was somehow missing out.

Saphia followed Vanda quietly and was so lost in her own thoughts that she barely noticed when Vanda stopped in front of a large store with big front windows.

'I reckon this is as good a place as any to start. Roftmun and Moans. They stock everything you could ever want and a few things you didn't know you wanted either,' said Vanda glancing back at her friend. 'Come along now. Do keep up Saphie.'

The pair entered the building in front of them. It was larger than the stores on either side. The front was white marble and the lettering over the blue door was in gold. Big display windows showed off all kinds of goods from food to jewellery as well as books and clothes. As soon as they entered Saphia once again noticed the effect Vanda had on people. She was like a flame attracting moths and they started to flutter towards her. One rather smartly dressed staff member headed straight for Vanda sweeping the others aside as if they weren't there.

'Vanda! Daaarling! It 'as been so long! You 'ave been ignoring us lately non? It is a terrible thing you do to neglect us 'ere at

Roftmun and Moans you know we will always do our very best to make you 'appy!' Following this was some air kissing.

Fairies air kiss by floating a little above the ground and making a show of kissing the cheeks of the fairy in front of them, first the left then the right. No contact is made however between cheek and lips. Following this the two fairies will tilt towards each other and gently touch the tips of their wings overhead as if bowing to each other before settling back down on the ground.

'Oh Yves! Things are so very busy these days! It's hard for a girl to find the time to shop at all!' said Vanda dramatically. 'I have not been neglecting you I have been neglecting everyone! I am so sorry but I shall make it up to you I promise. First though, I must introduce you to my lovely friend Saphia.' Vanda said as the pair came back down to earth

'Pleased to meet you,' said Saphia holding out her hand to shake hands in a more formal, less friendly greeting. Yves took the proffered hand and shook it while blatantly eyeing up the attire of Saphia.

'Enchanté mademoiselle! Any friend of Vanda is a friend of ours! It seems you 'ave come to us not a moment too soon non?! Why we will 'ave you transformed in a matter of moments. Come, come do not be shy with Yves why I work miracles every day.'

Yves turned and before either Vanda or Saphia had a chance to reply to him he swept past, in the opposite direction, the staff he had just brushed out of the way and Vanda and Saphia hurried along in his wake like ducklings following their mother.

'Vladi! Shingu! I need you two please! The rest of you back to work non!' added Yves and two more ducklings added themselves to his train of followers.

'Why do I get the feeling today that people aren't happy with my clothes.' Saphia said under her breath so that only Vanda could hear. This was really all rather insulting she thought.

'Just roll with it Saphie.' Vanda whispered back.

'This way we'll be in the private personal shopping area and we can talk in relative privacy with Yves. He knows who all the suppliers are and I know he will help us.'

'Well he'd better because I'm getting a little sick of being made to feel like a fairy in need of some kind of makeover. Which, by the way, I do not want or need.' Saphia added grumpily. She really was starting to regret coming along.

They continued through the shop passing all kinds of goods. Tables were piled high with scarves and hats, shelves displayed wing piercings and wing sleeves, they passed one area packed from the floor to the roof with glass beads and balloons that Saphia had to ask Vanda about.

'Oh they're the latest in home decor! They play music to match your mood I'm told. Personally I'm not sure that's such a good idea. I think they might be a fad.' Vanda told her.

Eventually they reached what could only be a private personal shopping area. It was quiet, they were alone, and there was virtually nothing there except mirrors, changing rooms and comfortable chairs placed about for people to lounge on. Lounging elegantly was not something Saphia felt she had the skill for. She felt out of place and not at all happy.

'Vladi! Shingu! You know what to do! Let's make this fairy shine!' declared Yves and he turned to her with his best smile.

'Indeed there is a lot to be done non? 'Owever we will prevail! We will find your 'idden princess under all that black oui?'

Vladi and Shingu scuttled off to do Yves bidding exiting the way they had just come and leaving the three of them alone.

Yves fussily escorted the ladies over to some seats and then went to fetch drinks for them. Saphia found herself sipping fizzy water with lemon in and was surprised to realise that it calmed her down a little.

'Yves you and I have known each other a long time haven't we?' Vanda asked. 'We have got to know a lot about each other and you are someone I both trust and admire and I think that you would not refuse me if I asked a favour of you?' Vanda brought Yves down to sit next to her on her sofa and looked him straight in the eyes.

'It is true. We 'ave know each other quite some time I am touched at your sentiment. What is this favour that you ask of Yves? 'Ow may I 'elp you?'

Before Vanda had the chance to answer Vladi and Shingu re-appeared with their arms laden down with clothes. None of them seemed to be black Saphia noticed. The clothes were taken behind one of the big red plush velvet curtains, the fizzy water removed from her hand and she was escorted politely, but firmly, to the changing room. To begin she was handed a royal blue dress with a matching jacket.

'Look I really don't have time for this. Can we not do this some other time?' she appealed to Vanda.

Vanda gave her a look of sharp look of frustration and wandered - actually she didn't wander she sashayed - toward her and whispered in her ear.

'If we want Yves to help us we will need to give him something in return. I am giving him you as a little project to keep him happy and at the same time this little ruse will allow us to talk undisturbed and in complete privacy. You need to just suffer through this I'm afraid dear Saphie. And you never know you may actually find something you like!'

With this said she turned on her heel and sashayed back to Yves who was lounging, most elegantly Saphia noticed, on the sofa.

Saphia dutifully tried on the dress. She hated it. It was too tight round the middle and too big on the sleeves and dragged along the floor. Unhappy, but playing along for now, she peered from behind the curtain before trying to walk out from the changing room towards Vanda. She did not get far.

'Oh la vache! Non! That is all wrong!' exclaimed Yves. 'It is not your fault mademoiselle it is these idiots 'ere.'

He rounded on his younger assistants. 'What were you thinking! You were not non! For the lady we need style! Class! Timeless elegance! This is not a lady who follows the fashion! She is a lady that glides on as fashion passes her by with its fads and whims. Try the baby blue and grey La Belle next!'

Saphia admitted to herself that she liked the sound of being outside fashion and yet classy. Maybe this man did know what he was talking about after all. She allowed herself to be shuffled back into the changing room where an alternative was offered. This was totally different and, Saphia had to admit, really did rather suit her. This time as she left the changing room she felt different. Like she was a woman who knew where she was going and what she was about. It was something she had never realised you could get from clothes.

'Ah! You see what I mean? This, this is so much better, it is a picture of elegance we see before us!' beamed Yves.

Saphia wasn't looking at Yves though she was looking at Vanda. Vanda's jaw had dropped. She was stood with her mouth hanging open in shock. Saying nothing she came over to Saphia and walked round her looking closely.

'Well what do you think?'

'I had no idea what you really looked liked! It's stunning. You are a different person. You simply have to buy it I'm afraid. Yves!' Vanda said turning to him, 'Carry on! We need to find out what we have really uncovered under all that black!'

Yves was still beaming and, now that Vladi and Shingu had got the message, they went to their task with gusto. This left Vanda free to talk to Yves while Saphia tried on what felt like more clothes in half an hour than she'd tried on her whole life.

'Yves I need to know where the fairy floss is coming from.' Vanda said bluntly as the pair returned to the sofa waiting for the next version of Saphia to be revealed. 'I need you to get the pair of us to wherever this is being made and we need to get there as soon as we can.'

'But why? This is not something you are interested in surely? It is a fad! It will be over in a few weeks and gone.'

'Because it should have been gone already! Haven't you noticed that it's been available for weeks? Haven't you noticed how people are eating a lot more of it than normal? Haven't you wondered why the prices are so low this year? This stuff is normally in short supply and expensive. Not this year though. I want to find out why.' Vanda explained.

'Well you are right,' said Yves slowly thinking through what she had said. 'Yes it does seem cheap. I do not eat it though as it would ruin my figure,' he said tapping his rather rotund stomach lightly, 'in fact now you mention it some of my staff seem, 'ow shall I say, a little more curvaceous than normal lately.'

'That's it exactly! People are getting sick Yves. Our friends are eating too much of this and it's not good for them. I want to know where it's coming from and I want to stop it. I need to know where it comes from. I have to see for myself so I can decide what to do next. Will you help me?'

'Of course I will 'elp you. You are my friend and I love the mystery and the intrigue! It is just like being back at 'ome with my brothers and sisters. This will be, 'ow you English say, easy as pie. We are one of zer biggest buyers, we 'ave deliveries every day. I can let you both tag along with our people. Pas de problème!'

Yves was clearly distracted while he spoke to Vanda and now he rose from his seat and opened his arms wide towards the changing room where Saphia had just emerged.

'Look! Look at the lovely Saphia! Incroyable! We have our princess!'

Saphia was dressed in a beautiful moss green suit in wool. It softened her features and gave her a glow. Gone was the harsh black that she had been hiding behind. Here was a beautiful fairy.

'I feel like a new person. It is beautiful and so soft and warm, it is just like wearing a hug! I can't help but smile wearing this. I feel like it was made just for me.'

Saphia came over to Vanda, who by now was also standing, and Yves. She hugged Yves tightly.

'Thank you,' she said simply. 'Thank you for showing me a different me that has been hiding all this time.'

Then she turned and hugged Vanda. 'You were right and I had no idea that clothes could change the way you feel about yourself. I always thought they were just things to cover you up. They aren't. They let you say things about yourself. They express your character. I feel some serious shopping coming on if you will help me?'

Vanda and Yves expressed delight at this new found Saphia and promised that they would help her continue finding her new self as soon as they could but they had something else to deal with first.

'Saphie darling Yves has said we can tag along with the staff who take the deliveries of fairy floss. I think we should go with them today. The sooner we get to the bottom of this the better and I am so over just thinking about this all the time.'

'That's fabulous thank you Yves! When do they leave?'

'In about 'alf an 'our,' he replied. 'But we will need to get you into our uniform, neither of you are exactly inconspicuous in those outfits.'

Shingu was sent off to another part of the store to get the girls the shop outfits. They changed quickly and were ready to go.

'Now please ladies do not do anything rash. Please promise Yves that you will just go and look and not touch this time?'

'We promise,' both of them chimed.

'We promise and will let you know what we find out too.' Vanda said.

Yves escorted the girls to the back of the shop where two other fairies were waiting to head out to collect the next fairy floss delivery.

'Please look after my precious girls you two!' said Yves, partly joking, 'we need them back in one piece.'

A disturbing discovery

Vanda and Saphia followed the other two fairies but kept quiet. They had decided that the fewer people who knew what they were up to the better as they didn't want to get anyone into any trouble if that's what it came too. Keeping quiet was something Vanda was not very good at but she tried hard all the same. She was still amazed on the inside as to the transformation of her friend when she had tried on the new clothes. She was already plotting ways to get her out more to surprise their old friends with her new look. Musing on this helped her keep her mouth shut.

Saphia was keeping quiet too but she was also focussed. She was remembering the route they were taking, paying attention to the people that passed them on the way and what they were carrying. She noted down a couple of 'suspicious' looking characters in her head for future reference and generally enjoyed the feeling of doing something practical that would hopefully help in the long run.

It wasn't too long until they came to a place with lots of big sheds. Like a sort of industrial estate for fairies. The only thing that made the shed they were going to different was it was pink. Most of the other sheds were dull blues or greys. This one was baby pink. There were no windows in any of the sheds except high up to let in a small amount of light. All the sheds had big doors so that large quantities of whatever was inside could be moved easily.

'So you two are just here to watch okay. Leave everything to us and just follow any instructions we give you.' One of the fairies with them, called Rimmer, spoke to them as they got to the big door.

'This won't take long at all. We're here to pick up a big delivery but because this stuff is so light it's easy to move between the two of us. We won't be asking for your help.'

'Fine by us,' replied Saphia.

The little group knocked on the big pink door and waited a moment before it was opened for them.

Rimmer spoke first. 'Good afternoon. We're from Roftmun and Moans for today's delivery. I have a docket here for ten large bags of fairy floss.'

He handed this over to rather ancient looking fairy who had opened the door and took it from him.

'Yup. We've been expecting you. Just wait a moment while I and go and get your order ready. It won't be long.' Off he went. He didn't check to see who the extra fairies were that had come along. He didn't seem interested.

While he was gone Vanda and Saphia took a moment to wander a little further into the shed. It was poorly lit so it was hard to see but there were large shelving units with lots of bags of fairy floss on them. They were all arranged by different sizes with the biggest bags on the bottom and the smallest at the top. It all looked very normal and there was nothing obviously suspicious to see.

'Do you think this is it?' asked a disappointed Vanda.

'No. No it can't be. This is just a distribution centre. The spider farm must be somewhere else.' Saphia replied.

Just then the fairy returned with ten huge bags of fairy floss floating behind him like pink clouds.

'Here you go then and take it with thanks we need the space. We can't get rid of this stuff fast enough. There's so much coming in every day I can barely keep up. I tell you it's never been like this. I've been in this business ninety two years and I've never seen anything like it. They must have hundreds of spiders. It's incredible.'

Saphia could help herself. 'So the spiders aren't here?' she asked.

'Good heavens no young 'un!' he replied. 'No, they need peace and quiet and fresh air and a good supply of nectar. You don't get that in a shed now do you! No they'll be down by the Skillith Beck if I'm any judge. Grand hedgerows there. There's something flowering most of the year. And it's quiet. Nobody to bother them neither. I remember in my youth going down to see how it was

68

done. Wasn't for me o'course but there you go. It was interesting enough now I think back on it.'

'What was it like?' Vanda asked encouragingly.

'Well it's quite hard to describe really if you've not seen it an all but I'll try. The spiders aren't that big. In fact they're quite cute to tell the truth. The biggest would fit from my elbow to my hand. They choose their own spot, spin a little web close to whatever flower they think is best and just sit there. Just sit there, being spiders doing spider things. So you have this hedgerow all covered in this fine spun silk. You have to wait for them to move on before you can take whatever silk they leave.'

He was getting into his stride now and seemed to be enjoying having an audience and someone to talk to.

'You see the spiders can re-use this silk unlike some. Its precious stuff right enough so you can't take it till they're done with it. I think I was told they leave it behind when they've mated and nested. Not all spiders wait to see how their babies get on you see. They leave before they hatch. So off they go after weaving a little place for the eggs but generally leaving the web that they were in. Now you don't touch the silk with the eggs. That would be a terrible thing. No point in collecting the silk from the egg case as you'd be destroying the chances of the next generation. That wouldn't just be bad for the spiders it'd be bad for us. If we damaged the young 'uns there wouldn't be enough spiders to spin silk next time and we'd never get fairy floss again.'

'So all we do is wait for them to move on and tidy up what's left for ourselves?' Saphia asked.

'Right you are young lady that's the truth. It's all very harmonious like. Think they use the words "sustainable agriculture" for it these days. We take what they leave. Recycling at its very best,' he smiled at his little audience.

'O'course this time around things seem a bit different I've thought.'

'What do you mean by that?' Saphia asked.

69

'Well it does seem to have lasted a while longer than I'm used to. Normally by now I'm off on my holidays to Cornwall to see my good lady wife's side of the family but we've had to put it off as things are still so busy. Not that I mind of course, it's a job and it pays well enough. The other thing that's odd is how much there is. Like I said, they must have hundreds of spiders down there. I've had to take on bigger premises this year to accommodate it all.'

'It does seem rather odd doesn't it,' Vanda said sweetly. 'You haven't thought of going down to the beck to see the spiders have you? Just to see what's going on out of curiosity or anything?'

'In truth no miss. I don't get out as much as I used to in my younger days. I'm not too fussed to be honest. I've seen it once already. No need to do it again. Not with my knees playing up like they do.'

'Ahh! Just as well you've come to take those bags away. Here comes the next lot behind you!' the fairy remarked.

Arriving at the shed were more bags. Lots more bags of fairy floss.

'Afternoon to you Size. Where do you want me to put these?' The question came from the one fairy who was marshalling the large number of fairy floss bags that were bobbing around like fluffy clouds trying to escape. He was right in the centre of them and now emerged for them to see. He was huge, a full nine inches tall and as big as a rock pipe player, maybe bigger. 'I see you have company?'

Vanda got straight to the point. 'We were just talking to Size here about the spiders. It all sounds so fascinating. I wonder if there's any chance of getting to see them?' she asked in her most ingratiating voice.

'No chance. I would stop thinking about that right now if I were you. No. There's nothing interesting about a bunch of spiders just hanging out in trees. Pretty boring really.'

'Now where am I putting these bags Size?'

'Right at the back of the shed if you wouldn't mind. There's a biggish space where these bags just came out of,' came the reply.

The large fairy pushed passed them with the bags of fairy floss. As he towed his bags past theirs it was like watching two groups of pink clouds fighting as some fought to stay still and others to move.

'Well thank you for your time Size,' said Saphia, 'we'd better get back now.'

'Ah it was lovely to have someone to talk to. I imagine I'll be seeing you all again soon enough,' Size replied.

Vanda and Saphia said nothing on the return journey to Roftmun and Moans. They had a lot to talk about once they'd left though and thankfully they didn't bump into Yves as they had nothing really to tell him.

'So how do you think that went?' Vanda asked.

'Well we didn't get to see the spiders which I suppose now really shouldn't be much of a surprise. Of course the operation wasn't going to be in a big shed somewhere. Whatever's going on Size isn't involved. He's a dear old thing isn't he. However that delivery guy? The one with the muscles? I wasn't sure if he was threatening us to stay away or just thought it wasn't that interesting. What do you think Vanda?'

'He was definitely trying to stop us. No doubt about it at all. I just know. I tell you what though. He doesn't know that Size told us where the spiders are likely to be. He won't be thinking that we'd know where to go. I reckon we go and have a look down by Skillith Beck tonight. What do you say? Up for an adventure?'

'Count me in. See you back at my place in two hours. I have some equipment I'll want to take. Do you think we should take anyone with us?'

'No we do this alone. But I think we should tell someone where we're going. I'll get messages to Hippy and Tattle.'

The two fairies parted company briefly while they got ready for their evening engagement.

When they met later it was fully dark and the place was much quieter. Fairies aren't that active in the evenings except for a few, the ones that work with fire flies, lightening bugs and glow worms and there aren't too many of them in Britain. Thankfully though, there was a full moon, so they had good light to see by.

'Right, I think I have everything.' Saphia was weighed down with a heavy bag.

'What on earth have you got in there?' Vanda asked.

'I'm going to record what we see so we can show the others.'

'Ohh! You have one of those new picapture thingies! I've heard about them. Never thought they'd be that useful myself. I can't see the point of looking at something once it's happened already.'

'I find it useful in my line of work to help me remember things after I've seen them. They are useful for capturing evidence when you want to show others later. Right! Enough chatting. Let's go shall we.'

Vanda and Saphia made their way north, down the hill past the old quarry where they had held the Highland Games, and then turned northwest to follow the base of the hill carrying on a downward slope the whole way. They moved out of the moonlit long grass into thicker bramble bushes and nettle patches as they went. The trees, mostly hawthorn and birch, started to get denser and they could hear a barn owl screeching somewhere nearby. Eventually, they heard the soft sound of a stream running over rocks and knew they were close to Skillith Beck. The light from the moon was still helpful even within the dense undergrowth and neither fairy felt that producing light themselves was a good idea. Who knew who was watching? Maybe guards had been placed around the spiders, they didn't know, and they didn't want to find out.

Moving as quietly as they could they proceeded cautiously forward towards the sound of the water running in the beck.

Saphia tapped Vanda on the shoulder and pointed above them and to the left. Vanda turned to look at what she had seen. It was a spider's web. Vanda nodded to indicate she'd seen it too and they stopped while Saphia got out her picapture as quietly as possible. She took a single picture of the web and, as the two stood stock still, they heard something moving close by.

Without panicking - which wouldn't have been much use - the two quietly ducked down as low as they could and waited. The noise came closer towards them and now they could see a fairy flying just above the top of the grass and nettles. What they could hear were his feet brushing the tops of the grass as he passed by. He wasn't looking their way at all. He was concentrating on the higher parts of the hedges and trees and he had a torch to see by that meant they could see him quite well. He looked just like the large well-muscled fairy they had met that afternoon at the pink shed. Exactly like him.

Feeling more confident that they weren't going to be spotted Saphia and Vanda waited for him to pass before standing back up from their hiding place.

'He might not be the only one Vanda. I think we must be close now. Do we carry on or go back? I don't want to bump into him out here at night do you?'

'We have to go on Saphie! We haven't found the spiders yet we'd have nothing to show for our visit to convince anybody of anything yet.'

Saphia nodded her agreement and now the two moved even more carefully and cautiously forward into the trees and hedges staying as low as they could until Vanda stopped dead in her tracks and grabbed Saphia's arm.

Saphia turned to look at her friend to see why she'd done that. Vanda was motionless and with eyes as big as saucers she was staring straight up above her. Saphia followed her gaze up to see whatever it was that had attracted Vanda's attention.

Above them was a spider. In fact it was a huge spider. Huge in the kind of way that made a girl think about spiders capable of catching and eating fairies. It sat in the middle of its web and appeared, thankfully, to be fast asleep. Because it was so dark they couldn't see it properly but what they could see was a massive body, with long legs and a menacing looking head. Saphia looked around to see if they were close to the edges of its web and it looked like they weren't. They were lucky they wouldn't trigger the fine silk of the web and cause the spider to wake. While she did this though her eye was drawn away from the first spider and she noticed another above this one, and then another off to the right, and another above it, and another...

...From where she was it looked like there must be hundreds of these huge spiders just in this small area. She couldn't help thinking that there were probably more she could not see. Remaining as calm as she could Saphia took some images with her picapture and hoped that there was enough light from the full moon to get some pictures of what they were seeing. She glanced sideways at Vanda who was standing as still as a statue transfixed apparently by the first spider.

'Vanda!' Saphia whispered, 'I think it's time we left now. We've seen what needed to and now we have to leave.'

Saphia took Vanda's hand and lead her back the way they came. Vanda passively followed her with the same fixed expression of shock on her face. Once again they had to wait for the guard fairy to pass by, this time in the other direction, and Saphia began to worry about her friend's silence. It was so unusual she wondered if Vanda had gone into shock. She led her all the way back to the clan entrance they'd left by and it wasn't until they reached it that Vanda spoke.

'She's bewitched the spiders! They aren't supposed to be that big! There aren't supposed to be that many! They shouldn't need guarding! They should be able to leave whenever they want! There's so much fairy floss because there are so many spiders and they're too big!'

Vanda turned to Saphia and anger and indignation shone like a beacon from her face. 'She is meddling with nature. It is so wrong, so very wrong. We have to do something Saphie!'

'We will Vanda, starting first thing tomorrow. Now though we both need rest. I will call everyone together in the morning. We are going to need help and we are going to need to show them what we've seen. I need some time to get the pictures from the picapture. I don't think anyone will argue that there isn't a need to do something after this.'

The two parted company and returned to their respective homes. Neither slept well though. Vanda was brimming with indignant energy to just go out and confront Gula but knew that that would be foolish so she spent a restless night imagining what she would do to her if there were no consequences. Saphia spent her night getting pictures of the spiders from the picapture ready and comparing the details of them to what she'd found in books. As the night wore on she got just as mad as Vanda.

Time for action

In the morning Saphia messaged Vanda, Tattle, Hippy and Yves as soon as she thought they would all be awake. She sent them instructions to meet by eight o'clock in the library where she had booked a room for them to meet in private. Saphia arrived first so she could be organised and ready to share what she had found with the others. She pulled down all the blinds in the room to make sure no one could see in and placed two images on a wall. One was of the first big spider they had seen and the second, of lower quality because of the poor light, showed a large number of spiders in the background. She had also numbered all the spiders in this image by hand coming to a total of forty one.

It was this picture she was studying while drinking coffee when Vanda arrived.

'Oh my goodness!' she exclaimed when she saw the second image, 'I'm so glad I didn't realise how many there were last night. I think I only saw the first one and then my mind sort of went a bit blank.'

'I did notice you were a bit distracted. This is just how many fit in this one picture. There must have easily been five or ten times this number.' Saphia said, 'It's a truly terrible thing that they've done.'

Saphia and Vanda didn't want to get too far into a discussion until the others showed up so they left the room and waited outside for everyone to arrive and quietly drank coffee and tried to wake up. They were both feeling exhausted but determined too.

Yves and Hippy arrived at the same time. Tattle was the last to arrive and looked like she had come straight from the gym as she was flustered.

'Sorry all. I've been running so many classes these days! I have never been busier I swear. I think the Highland Games experience really frightened a few people. The gym has been packed morning, noon and night. I know it's great but I'm exhausted all the time. Does anyone have anything to eat?'

'There's coffee and muffins inside,' Saphia said. 'Thanks all for coming as such short notice. Now before you go in can I please ask that when you enter the room you say nothing and just sit? It's probably going to be a shock.'

Tattle, Yves and Hippy glanced at each other with mild concern but went in with Saphia and Vanda bringing up the rear.

The pictures on the wall were enough to make them all sit down anyway. None of them seemed too interested in talking, they just stared. Tattle distractedly reached for coffee and two of the muffins. Hippy bounced back up from his seat to study the picture of the spider by itself. Yves just sat and stared.

Saphia brought them all up to speed on the story so far thanking Yves for his assistance in getting them to the shed where the fairy floss was distributed and explaining how they had acted as soon as they could once they'd had the information about where the spiders were.

'So now we know. I checked some books when I got home last night and the spiders seem to be ten time larger than the spiders we normally get fairy floss from. There can't be a mistake because there's only one kind of spider that produces fairy floss. This means we also know that they have been changed, or mutated, or something, because they are much, much bigger than they should be. Simply put a bigger spider produces a bigger web which means more fairy floss.'

There was a stunned silence. Tattle distractedly pushed muffin crumbs around the table. Hippy kept standing up to look at the pictures and then sitting down again. Yves looked thoughtful and was the first to speak. His voice came out slowly, like he was considering each of his words carefully before saying them.

'In all my years I 'ave never seen such a thing. It makes me ashamed to be a fairy. These creatures 'ave been turned against their nature for our purposes! For the pursuit of profit and gain and we 'ave allowed it to 'appen under our very noses!' He stood up from the table and walked to the picture of many spiders.

'We 'are all responsible for this. We should 'ave questioned this sooner! We should have asked why is the fairy floss so plentiful? Why is it so cheap? But non! We did not think to ask we just took the money and closed our minds to what it may mean!'

He turned to the others, 'We 'ave to tell people! This cannot go on! I will be cancelling all new orders for fairy floss and I will be telling people why. And when I tell people something I can assure you that they 'ear it!' he took a deep breath before carrying on.

'We can stop this now! Today! No more of this monstrous fairy floss at Roftmun and Moans! And where we lead others will follow!'

When he had finished he looked to the others for their approval. Vanda and Tattle looked excited and clapped their hands in agreement and Yves beamed at them.

Hippy and Saphia on the other hand did not look so convinced.

'Much as I admire your commitment and desire for action Yves,' said Hippy. 'I see a problem with your plan.' He sighed deeply and took his time standing, taking a long look at the spiders in the picture, before continuing.

'While I am heartened that Tattle's gym classes are doing well and it seems there are some who are changing their ways; we in the medical community are seeing a different attitude. There are fairies who we suspect will not give up the fairy floss even knowing that they are damaging themself by continuing to consume it. I am afraid that they have become addicted. This means as long as there is a demand there will be a supply. If the spiders are guarded and unable to leave, as Saphia has told us, the supply will continue. Even if Roftmun and Moans stopped stocking it, and they persuaded many others to stop too, it would only move the market elsewhere. There are always those who are willing to prey on the weaknesses of others. An addict will find a way. All that would happen if you stopped selling it would be a change of supplier.'

He sat down again heavily. 'No I think the only way we will resolve this is to somehow free the spiders. And not in their present form either, they need also to be returned to their original size, I personally find it very distressing that there are fairies who are prepared to physically alter other creatures for their own advantage.'

'I agree,' said Saphia. 'This has gone way beyond what we originally suspected. This is bigger than sorting out some personal vendetta against our clan. We cannot allow the perpetrator of this crime against nature – against our nature – to get away with the altering of another animal in such a horrendous way. We have to return the spiders to their original form and release them and if we can punish those responsible. Just stopping selling the fairy floss is not enough.'

'Alright, I take your point.' Yves said, 'But surely we can begin to make it 'arder by refusing to sell it and encouraging others to do the likewise?'

Tattle and Vanda nodded their agreement to Yves suggestion however again Saphia again disagreed.

'I'm sorry Yves. I admire your commitment and zeal in all this I really do. However, I'm afraid if you stop selling fairy floss it may be obvious to the people we want to catch that someone is on to them. It could make our job much harder if suspicions are aroused. They may step up security or move the spiders to a new site that we'd then need to find. We need to think this through carefully and know that when we act we will succeed. I think we may only get one chance.'

Saphia held Yves hands in her own and spoke gently to him as she tried to explain.

'You have to carry on selling fairy floss Yves. We need to find a way to make this whole horrible business end as soon as possible and we need you to carry on as normal in the meantime. Can you do that please?'

Yves could be seen to be struggling with his conscience. 'You are right but I do not like it. Non! I do not like it one little bit. This plan? We 'ad better come up with it fast because I do not know 'ow long I will be able to keep quiet. You understand me too?'

'Yes we understand Yves. Thank you.' Saphia gave him a little kiss on his cheek and he blushed as red as a rose.

'So we need a plan,' said Vanda. 'We need a plan to get those spiders out of there and fast and I think I know how we can do it.' She turned to the rest of them with a big smile.

'The spiders may be big but we know bigger people than the guards that surround them. I propose now is the time to tell Sarah and Emma what is going on. I doubt any fairy would be able to stop a human if they came to move the spiders.'

'Oh my goodness!' exclaimed Saphia, 'That's brilliant Vanda!'

'Yes it is isn't it.' Vanda replied with a huge smile on her face. 'Do you all want to come with us while we tell them?'

'Of course, but can we please have breakfast first. I'm still starving,' said Tattle. 'And I think that Yves could do with something too to settle his nerves before he meets his first humans!'

The gang of five, ready to fight the fairy floss, left the library arm in arm with buoyant spirits feeling ready to finally take some action. Vanda was proud of how well they'd done and how far they'd come in such a short time. She was also secretly pleased at how well she'd coped too. She was terrified of spiders and to have been so close to one that big, even it if was a vegetarian, last night had been to face one of her biggest fears. She felt proud that she'd got through that and now it looked like they would be doing something good for everyone she knew and cared about. Today was looking like a good day.

'I wish you wouldn't do that sometimes! It's lovely to see you and everything but isn't there any way you can warn me when you're about to pop into existence like that?' Sarah exclaimed.

Sarah was out in the garden at her Aunt Jane's cottage and Bertie was asleep near her in a warm patch of sunlight on the grass. Sarah was sat on a small stool with a painting easel in front of her. She was trying to paint a pink rose bush in front of her and had been rather pleased with her efforts of the morning right up to the moment Vanda had appeared. Having just loaded up her paint brush with pink paint the shock of Vanda appearing had caused her to draw a thick diagonal line of it across the whole canvas. She was not happy.

'Oh that's rather different isn't it?' said Vanda critically appraising the picture. 'Never mind, I'm sure you'll get better with practice. Anyway I'm not here to talk painting. We need to talk to you and Emma. Can you find her and meet by the hawthorn trees past the gate that leads to the field with the quarry in? Say half an hour?'

'I can try. I don't know what Emma's doing today but if I leave now we should be able to make it. Is it about the fairy floss? Have you found something? Was it the Gula person you were going to see?'

'Oh you are so far behind! So much has happened since the Games! Be quick! I'll get the others and see you soon,' and off she vanished.

Looking disappointedly at her painting Sarah quickly packed up her things and took them inside before heading off at a run to the Fawcett's farm up the lane. Thankfully, Emma was in and wasn't doing anything important. The two of them just got to the gate and trees within the half an hour deadline.

'So they've got something to show us have they?' Emma asked.

'I don't know really. Vanda just seemed very anxious to meet as soon as possible. You know as much as me.'

As she spoke the five fairies popped into view. What followed was a conversation that was hard to follow for Sarah and Emma. The five fairies, including a new one called Yves who seemed to have a French accent, were all talking across each other in their haste to get the story told. It was very hard to get a coherent story but eventually the girls managed to piece enough together from the group to get a good idea of what had been going on since they had last spoken. Emma tried to summarise counting out the main points on her fingers.

'So first you're saying Gula really is a baddy. Second, she doesn't care that she's doing this. Third, Yves somehow got you to someone who told you where the spiders were. Fourth, Vanda and Saphia went to see them and fifth they're bigger than they should be? In fact lots bigger than they should be so big we should be calling them mutants. And lastly you now need our help getting them released because they're under guard. Is that about right?'

The fairies nodded their agreement. 'Mostly yes,' said Saphia. 'And look we have pictures to prove it.'

She produced the two pictures she had shown the others earlier and, mumbling a few words over them, as Vanda had done with the Fabulous Fairy magazine, they grew in size so that the girls could make out what was on them. They had to admit they were certainly spiders and that there were quite a lot of them it would seem. It was however hard to tell how big they were.

'I hate spiders.' Sarah said, 'It's the way they move. I know they aren't dangerous and these are supposed to be vegetarian but I still don't like them much.'

'I quite like them,' replied Emma 'they do a really useful job of keeping flies and aphids down in the garden according to my granny. Just because they have eight legs isn't a reason to discriminate against them she says.'

'So you will help us?' asked Vanda 'It was my idea that you could collect and release all the spiders as the guards won't dare show themselves to humans. We know exactly where they are and we could go right now. This could all be over before the end of the day.' Vanda was rushing ahead of herself now as she could see the finish line in front of her but there was always the voice of reason in the form of Saphia to dampen her enthusiasm.

'The spiders Vanda. Think of the spiders. They have been changed into monsters! They are too big and if we release them they may die because something is keeping them that big. Or they may have babies that are massive and that would change the local ecosystem. We can't just let them go it could be bad for more than just the spiders. We need to fix what has been done to them. We need someone to undo this horrible mutation.'

'In the meantime though we can certainly collect as many of the spiders as we can can't we? While you find someone who can sort out the size of them?' asked Emma.

It was clear that the five fairies didn't know what to say. Vanda looked frustrated and disappointed, Saphia was staring at the ground avoiding eye contact with her friend, Tattle was pacing up and down with nervous energy clearly radiating off her. Yves and Hippy were huddled together speaking in voices so low they couldn't be heard but they looked like they were arguing. For a time no one said anything at all and Emma and Sarah waited patiently for some kind of answer. Eventually it was Yves who spoke out.

'Yes you can collect them. There ez someone who may be able to 'elp us but 'Ippy and I think it is very unlikely that 'e will.' He sighed heavily and glanced at Hippy who indicated that he should continue but his body language said he was not in full agreement at all. Yves sat down heavily on a rock and continued.

'The ladies 'ere are all too young to remember 'im. It was before they were born that we had a brilliant mind 'ere in the clan. A savant maybe you humans would 'ave called 'im. Many gifts and talents 'ad been given to 'im when he was born and 'e was considered the finest mind in a generation. 'Owever, his gifts and talents did not come without costs to other parts of his personality.' Yves looked to Hippy to take up the story which he did with great reluctance.

'Savant is the right word. He was exceptional in every regard. Any skill he tried he became expert at in a matter of days. No task was too hard, no occupation to difficult for him to master theoretically or practically. The problem was he had no abilities with people. He could not relate to, or understand, others emotions and feelings. He did not comprehend that we are all different, he could not appreciate the failings and problems of other fairies. Not even his parents and siblings. He found no friends at school and because he could not relate to others he became increasingly isolated. Many years ago he chose to totally shun all company and now lives as a hermit. By himself he studies whatever he is interested in and is, by all accounts, happy. His family make sure he has the basic things he needs having food and supplies delivered to him but he no longer communicates with anyone. We don't really know how he is or whether he would even consider the spider's a task appropriate to his intellect. It is more than likely he would simply turn us away. He has been asked in the past with no luck. His isolation seems to be self-inflicted and complete.'

Saphia, Tattle and Vanda looked completely surprised. Clearly they had never heard of such a person before.

Saphia was the first to speak. 'So we have in our midst's a rare talent and I am not aware of this person? When we have such a brain shouldn't we have worked harder to try and understand him before allowing him to give up on us? Imagine the good he could do?' she spoke accusingly now at Yves and Hippy.

Yves stared hard at the ground in front of him and his shoulders slumped forward in defeat.

'Ahh Saphie, you will not understand 'ow 'ard we tried. 'E chose a life for 'imself away from the rest of us. To 'ave tried any 'arder would have been to torment 'im.' Yves replied with great sadness.

'Well if he is our only idea for now then we have to go and see him.' Tattle spoke up for the first time and she had a determined expression on her face. 'We have to go and see him and we will make him understand how important it is that he helps. Just because he has chosen to live away from us does not mean that he isn't still part of the community! Where does he live? We need to get there as soon as we can because from what you're saying it could be quite an effort to get him on our side so we'd better start sooner rather than later.'

'We can take you to his home that is not a problem. However, I would prepare yourselves to be disappointed,' said Hippy.

'I think I know how we can try and make him help us though,' piped up Saphia with a glint in her eye.

'I think Vanda is right that Sarah and Emma should go and collect the spiders. I think if anyone who knows as much as you claim he does were to see what had been done to them they would have to help. It's against nature and I can't help thinking the spiders are suffering. If we can show him one of these creatures maybe, and importantly, his academic curiosity will be stirred to action. That could be our way in. A problem that no one else can solve. Something so unnatural and wrong. Wouldn't any expert or scholar want to help if they could?'

'Or maybe they'd want to show off that they could do something no one else could do?' said Vanda. 'I like it Saphia. It's a little bit cunning,' added Vanda whilst giving her friend a hug.

'So how is this going to work?' asked Emma. 'Someone shows us where you found the spiders. We collect them in the safe knowledge that no fairies guarding them would dare tackle humans. In the meantime the others go and find this genius fairy. What is his name anyway? And try and persuade him to at least listen to what we have to say. If that doesn't work we turn up with the spiders and hope his academic curiosity and brilliance takes over and helps anyway.'

'Can I again just point out that I hate spiders?' said Sarah in a small voice, 'I really, really don't like them and I'm not sure how much use I'm going to be for this bit. Can't we get someone to help? There are loads of them in that photo of yours Saphia which I guess means there are even more of them in reality. I'm not happy about having to collect them at all. In fact the chances are I'll end of squashing them out of panic.'

'Ben. My brother Ben. We could bring him in on this. You know how good he is with animals Sarah. He's only five but he's just so into them. Remember how well he looked after Del before we could get him fixed?'

Sarah thought back to the day they had encountered a fairy that had been turned into a wood duck that had got its wing broken. It had turned out for the best in the end but Ben had done all he could to help the duck not knowing that in fact it was a fairy. It would mean telling someone else about the fairies and he was only five. Could he be trusted with such a big secret she wondered?

As if she was reading her mind Emma cut in, 'No one would ever believe him if he said he'd seen fairies you know that don't you? What five year old boy would ever tell anyone he'd seen fairies. Can you imagine what his elder brothers would say if he told them?'

Emma and Ben had two older twin brothers called Simon and Jon. Sarah couldn't visualise Ben ever telling his brothers such a secret they would only laugh at him and call him a silly baby. She felt pretty sure that Emma had made a great point.

Hippy broke into her thoughts. 'His name is Cereb to answer your question Emma. I think that all of us except you two and Vanda should head to his home now. Vanda can show you where the spiders can be found and once we have tried to speak to him we can meet again. Saphia's idea is a good one. I do not think that argument alone will be enough to get him on our side.'

'And I think that your petit frère sounds like a perfect new addition to our gang Emma. We men are 'eavily outnumbered as it is and would welcome 'im most warmly non,' said Yves looking at Hippy for support.

'Well off you all go then,' said Vanda. 'We have important work to be getting on with and, in our case, sooner seems best if only because Sarah looks positively ill at the idea of spiders.'

Sarah did in fact look quite pale and said nothing as Yves, Hippy, Tattle and Saphia vanished from sight leaving her with

Emma and Vanda to try and cheer her up as they walked back towards the farm to get Ben and a lot of containers for spiders.

Ben joins the 'Free Fairies From Floss' team

As they walked back to the farm Emma and Sarah tried to come up with the best way to break it to Ben about the fairies and the spiders. It was fair to say that they didn't come up with any good ideas before they got there.

'I give up. How on earth are we going to try and get him to understand Emma?'

'I have no idea, I really don't. Other than just telling him and seeing what happens next I'm all out of brilliant ideas. There is no way he'll believe us. He'll laugh at us just as we would laugh at him.'

Vanda had listened, as patiently as she could, but finally had enough. 'Look how about you just tell him. I appear and introduce myself, generally behave like something out a story book and then we can get on with what we came to do? Hmm? Think that'll work? Because I know it will.' She fluttered and spun in front of Sarah and Emma giving off the impression that she had had quite enough of listening to their nonsense when there was a perfectly obvious way to proceed.

'I think she might have a point Sarah. What do you think?'

'Yeah. Reckon that'll just about do it.'

They found Ben playing with a couple of the farm dogs in the big barn next to the house. He was throwing sticks for them and the dogs were racing each other to be the first to retrieve them.

'Where have you two been? Not that I'm complaining but I've hardly seen my sister lately.' Ben giggled. He said this surrounded by the dogs barking and wagging their tails wanting the game to continue.

'We've been sort of busy with something and now we think that you'd like to know what it is too. But, I need you to just listen to me while I tell you this and then you can ask questions if you like,' said

Emma. 'You see there have been some quite odd things happening lately and, well...'

Emma told Ben everything starting from the beginning and he listened, like he was told, all the way through till the end. '...and of course we'd like you to meet Vanda.'

'Blimey.' It was all Ben could say when faced with something that looked like it belonged on top of a Christmas tree dancing about in front of his face wafting a sparkly wand and giggling. It seemed that Vanda had had time to find something to change into to complete the overall story book effect she was after. He would later describe their meeting as rather like being harassed by a flying pink meringue.

'Fairies getting fat on fairy floss made from spiders webs? Mutant spiders under armed guard? If it wasn't for this one here making me feel a bit hungry floating about like a cake I'd say you'd gone a bit bonkers sis. On the other hand what if you're not making it up? I'd miss out on mutated massive spiders and that's just not happening.'

He took off towards the house like a rocket with the dogs still on his heels wondering if playtime was still happening. Following closely behind the dogs were the girls.

'What are you doing?' called Emma.

'Well first I'm getting a pair of gloves in case they bite and then I'm getting a lot of Tupperware boxes that mum won't miss to put all these spiders in. I can't believe you haven't got them already.'

Emma, Sarah and Vanda waited outside for Ben.

'Well that seemed to go remarkably well. He seems to have taken it all in his stride,' said Vanda.

'Yeah. But then I shouldn't be surprised really, he's my brother and he's always been a bit odd. Odd in a good way I mean,' said Sarah when the other two looked at her questioningly.

'Right! I'm ready, let's go.' Ben said as he emerged from the house carrying a bag full of plastic boxes and wearing a pair of gardening gloves that looked a little too big for him.

Making sure that they weren't seen by anyone in the house, after all the route took them past the out-of-bounds quarry, they followed the pink puffball that was Vanda down to the beck and the bramble, birch and hawthorn tangle of trees and hedgerow that grew along the banks. Just as they arrived Vanda got them to stop while she pointed out where she and Saphia had been the night before and then excused herself. It wouldn't be a good idea for her to be seen there with them just in case.

'Thank you all so much for this. Get as many of the poor things as you can and please be careful with them. I'm going to find the others now to find out how they are getting on with Cereb. And don't be scared Sarah dear. They are vegetarians after all,' and with that Vanda placed a light kiss on Sarah's forehead for luck and promptly vanished.

'I hate spiders,' said Sarah quietly to herself. 'No one seems to be listening to me though so we might as well get on with it.'

Ben was placing some grass, twigs and some flowers he'd found in a few of the boxes. 'They'll need something to eat and to hang on to,' he said when he saw their questioning looks.

'Sarah, why don't you hold the boxes at the bottom and Emma and I can collect them and put them in so you don't have to touch them okay?'

Sarah nodded her consent unenthusiastically and dumbly took one of the containers from him holding it out in front of her at arm's length with her eyes closed so she couldn't see. Emma and Ben gently collected the spiders, they were about the size of a ten pence piece, and put them in the boxes. Ben seemed somewhat disappointed that they were not bigger. Once they had a few spiders in a box they would swop over to a new box and carry on collecting. There seemed to be a lot of them and Sarah wasn't finding it easy although she did feel some relief whenever she got to put the lid on a box.

After what must have been a good hour of spider collecting Sarah was told she could put the final lid on the one she was holding as it was the last one.

'We've got as many of them as we can for the moment,' said Ben. 'We can come back tomorrow to check as we're bound to have missed a few. They're really pretty aren't they!' he exclaimed as he gently placed the last of the spiders in the box.

'I wonder where the guards are that Saphia and Vanda saw?' Emma said. 'I know we weren't expecting any problems from them but it just seems really odd that we haven't seen anything or heard anything.'

'I guess they just weren't expecting humans to be here at all. I mean why would you? We aren't even supposed to know fairies exist so why would they plan for us being involved? Chances are we've terrified them and they've taken off somewhere,' replied Sarah as she sat down some distance from the containers with the spiders in, relieved that it was all over, for today at least.

Ben picked up one of the containers and took one of the spiders out to have a proper look at it.

'I can't believe it's a mutant though. Just looks like a regular spider to me. Maybe a little bigger than normal and browner, not like the house spiders we get in doors, and they have amazing green eyes!' he carefully placed the spider back in the box.

'So these guys spin a web that tastes like candy floss right?' he asked no one in particular.

'Yeah that's right,' said Emma, Sarah wasn't in the mood for talking, and didn't respond at all. 'Why are you going to try some and find out?'

'Brill idea sis!' grinned Ben. He broke off a small birch twig from a tree beside him and approached the place they'd been taking the spider from. There were quite a few webs and he carefully wrapped them around the end of the twig. There wasn't much to look at when he'd finished, in human terms anyway, but there was a little piece of ever so slightly pink fluff on the end of his twig. He gently picked at it with his fingers and placed a bit in his mouth while his sister looked.

Ben smacked his lips together as he thought about the flavour.

'It's not very obvious to me. What do you think?' and he held out his twig to his sister Emma.

'We got to try it before thanks I don't need to try again. You can have it.'

'Suit yourself then,' and Ben tried a little more of the web. 'Maybe, yeah, hang on a minute, it is a bit sweet. No seriously you should try it,' once again he held out the twig to Emma.

She took it off him and extracted a tiny piece from the end and placed it on her tongue. Initially she said nothing while she waited for it to melt. Then she took a little bit more of the web and tried again.

'Oh it's sweeter when it's fresher! It's a bit like honey! Sarah do you want to try it? It's nicer than the stuff Sivle gave us!'

Sarah, who had a bit of a thing for sweets, momentarily forgot about the spiders and joined to other two in sampling the webs-on-a-stick.

'It's just like honey! I think it's much nicer than candyfloss as it's not so sticky and artificial don't you think? We should probably stop though as we may have rescued the spiders but if we eat all the webs too it may cause problems we don't want later.'

Ben didn't really want to stop eating now he'd discovered, what he called the honey webs, but the girls persuaded him they really should be getting back to the farm now. With both her youngest children missing Kathryn, Ben and Emma's mum, might be starting to worry a bit about what they were up too. So they collected up all the containers, which seemed to contain an awful lot of spiders, and made their way back to the farm.

The spiders were hidden in one of the lofts in an out building and Ben took it upon himself to look after them, not that that really meant doing much at all, and in the meantime they just had to wait to find out how the others were getting on.

'I hate not knowing what's happening,' said Emma, 'I feel left out and I want to know how they are getting on with this Cereb fairy. Do you think he'll help?'

'I have no idea,' replied Sarah, 'but I hope that he's going to help and I know that if Vanda and Tattle get the chance to be all enthusiastic at him it should be pretty much a done deal. Those two don't exactly take no for an answer when they've decided something do they?' she grinned at Emma and the pair of them laughed when they thought of the join persuasive powers of Vanda and Tattle.

'In the meantime I'm off home as it's getting late and Aunt Jane will wonder where I've been. I guess I'll see you two tomorrow to round up any spiders we missed and hopefully Vanda and the others will be around to tell us how they've got on.'

Sarah left the others and walked down the lane to her Aunt's cottage thinking about everything that had happened that day. It had certainly been unusual and she never would have guessed it would have involved kidnapping, or maybe she should call it rescuing, mutant spiders. Why they'd rescued them, who from and what for, remained to be seen and it certainly gave her something to think about in the evening.

Cereb's decision?

In the meantime, while the children rescued the spiders, Saphia, Tattle, Hippy and Yves had gone on a mission to try and persuade a fairy called Cereb to help them change the spiders back to their normal size.

'I cannot tell you ladies how small I think our chances are of persuading Cereb to our point of view,' said Hippy. He was very unhappy with this plan as he really believed there was no chance of it working and he was trying to let Saphia and Tattle know so they wouldn't be too disappointed when they were let down. He was also unhappy because he knew that if it did not work they had no backup plan either. They hadn't come up with an alternative way of restoring the spiders to their original size if Cereb decided not to help.

''Ave a little faith doctor 'Ippy. If we do not try we will never know.' Yves was just as unhappy as Hippy but he was always in possession of an optimistic view of life and so was not considering the possibility of failure. He was determined to make this idea work especially as he did not want to fail in front of Saphia of whom he had become quite fond.

Hippy got them to halt just before they reached the isolated place where Cereb lived. He had something to say.

'I would prefer it if you left me to do the talking. I knew Cereb a little when we were both younger and it may be that he will listen to me rather than any of you before he decides, most likely, to turn us down anyway. Are you all okay with that?'

'Fine by us but don't expect me to remain silent if he refuses when he can obviously help,' replied Saphia. 'I struggle with the idea that that someone with the talents you describe should lock themselves away from the world rather than helping. It's just wrong.'

'Try Saphie darling,' said Tattle. 'We all have our differences and we all need to respect each other for them. If he won't help we can't bully him into it.'

'Exactly Tattle. Thank you.' Hippy turned and knocked on the door with the others lined up closely behind him waiting to see if the elusive Cereb would even answer. Nothing happened so after a minute or so Hippy tried again. Saphia was starting to get restless and so Hippy knocked for a third time and stuck his ear to the door to hear if there was any noise betraying the presence of someone inside.

'I can hear someone in there,' he whispered to the others, 'I'm going to try one more time.'

This time something happened. Hippy could hear quiet footsteps in the hallway that eventually rather slowly reached the door and it opened the tiniest of cracks. Saphia, Tattle and Yves strained to see past Hippy and inside but they could see nothing. It was completely dark and they couldn't even make out the shape of a fairy's head peering at them from the safety of the doorway.

'Hello Cereb. It's me Hippy. Do you remember? It's been a little while since we talked as I know how you like your privacy but I would like to talk to you now.'

The softest voice spoke back from the hidden figure behind the door and all four of them had to strain to make out what was said.

'Why do you bother me? Why did you come here Hippy? I remember you of course I do! I have a brain that remembers everything and forgets nothing so why are you filling it now with useless chatter? Go away. You know as well as anyone that I see no one and I talk to no one.' And just like that the voice abruptly stopped and the door closed.

Hippy however wasn't quite ready to give up and knowing that Cereb was there by the door, as he hadn't heard retreating footsteps, spoke anyway.

'Please Cereb. Please speak with me. You know I respect your privacy and so you know that I would not come unless it was with very good reason. I have a reason, I have an urgent need – we all have an urgent need – of your help. I can think of no one who's knowledge, talent and intellect surpasses yours. There is no one who can help if you cannot and if you refuse to hear me out I believe people will die. Deaths which I believe you can prevent if you would apply yourself to our problem. Please Cereb. Please listen to me.'

The door remained closed but Hippy indicated to the others to remain quiet. He had not heard footsteps retreating from the door and he was hopeful that Cereb was considering what he'd said. There was complete silence; no sound came from behind the door and the others tried hard to breathe quietly too. Hippy took a deep breath and began to talk to the door hoping that Cereb was still there and was listening.

He talked through the changes in the fairies since the fairy floss had become cheap and plentiful, he talked about the changes he'd seen in friends and the injuries at the Highland Games. He talked to the door about Gula and her claiming responsibility for the supply of fairy floss but not her responsibility to its consequences. Then he talked about Vanda and Saphia's trip to the beck that night where they had seen the spiders and their guards. He told, the still firmly shut door, about the plan to capture the spiders and about how it was probably happening right now and then he talked about how Cereb was the only one they thought could help.

'You should see the spiders Cereb. It's against nature what has been done to them. They are transformed and they are trapped just as you probably felt trapped by us when we tried to make you fit in with the rest of us. You chose isolation, a life on your own, but still close to us. These spiders have had their lives, and their choice taken, they have no choice but to spin webs of floss and live in bodies too big for them. Is there nothing I can say that will make you even talk to us? To suggest something we can do? Please Cereb.'

96

Hippy rested both hands and his forehead against the door with nothing but hope that there was someone on the other side listening.

Saphia, as quietly as she could, crept up to the door beside Hippy. She took from her bag the two picapture prints of the spiders she had put up on the library wall and slid them silently under the door. She thought she sensed other hands pulling them in from the other side and smiled. She waited silently next to Hippy with the others equally quiet behind them. You could have heard a flower bloom they were so still.

'These images. I will talk to the one who took them.'

They hadn't waited long at all. Saphia's idea to appeal to his intellectual curiosity may have worked. The door opened a fraction, revealing a hallway behind it that was now lit, along with the fairy called Cereb. He spoke so quietly it was as if he was afraid of using up his voice if he talked louder.

'That would be me,' said Saphia. 'I am sorry to intrude on your peace but we want to ask you to solve a puzzle that no one else can. If you do indeed have the mind I have been told you have then this may be a challenge even for you. I presume knowledge, puzzle solving and curiosity are what ultimately drive you?'

Cereb laughed and it was a small tinkling sound that did not seem to come easily. 'Not quite that but something like that. Please come in.'

He held the door open and Saphia entered. Hippy moved to follow her but found the door closed quickly behind Saphia shutting the rest of them out. He realised the rest of them would just have to wait and took a seat on the doorstep. Inside the home Saphia followed Cereb down a hallway that had many closed doors off to each side. The hall ended in the kitchen, or at least she guessed it was the kitchen, as it had a sink and table and lots of other things expected of a kitchen but lots of unexpected things too. There were glass jars full of odd looking plants, bubbling pots on the stove and strange looking instruments hanging from the ceiling. Instead of being nosey and asking what they were for she decided to hold her tongue. Here was someone who had no need of other people. Undoubtedly he would be offended, and possibly ask her to leave, if she pried too much into his life when they had just met. So she waited for him to speak first.

Cereb sat at the table and began to talk. He barely looked at Saphia who had, uninvited, taken a seat opposite him. In order to hear his soft manner of speaking she had to lean towards him to make out his words.

'I heard what Hippy said. Understand that I do not care what people do to themselves. It is their decision what they do each day when they wake up. Who they see, what they eat and drink and what they do. We are responsible for ourselves and I believe in the principle of non-harm. We all have power. We can choose to use that power however we want unless we intend harm to others. I will not harm any fairy but if the tale Hippy related to me is true, and if these images are real, then harm has been intentional. This is a use of power against our commonly accepted societal norms and I agree that in principle such an action deserves an opposite reaction if at all possible.'

As he continued to speak the volume and emotion in his voice rose until he was almost speaking at an ordinary volume. Saphia began to feel hopeful that he would help but she was nervous of speaking in case she upset his train of thought.

'However, I am not a judge or jury. Nor do you or I have the backing of our society to act on its behalf. So we do not have the right to intervene even when harm is clearly being done. I have no right to restrict another fairy's liberty and freedom to act. There is always recourse for reasoning with the perpetrator with the hope of a change in their behaviour. However, I understand two of you have already tried this with no success. There is no value in someone else trying the same arguments and I certainly have no appetite to try. Therefore I cannot help.'

He turned his eyes, which were the deepest, darkest brown held in a face with skin white as snow, hidden behind a greying mop of hair and beard to Saphia.

'I am sorry but you should leave now.'

Saphia was dumbstruck. It had sounded as though he would at least consider helping seconds ago and now he was blankly refusing? Her mind raced to produce something to make him think again.

'I understand that no fairy has the right to make decisions for another. However we live within a community, we all live within the rules and norms that govern it. I do not stay up at night until five in the morning practicing the rock pipes because I know my neighbours need sleep and it would be unfair and unsociable! This fairy, Gula, has of her own choosing come back to our community. To me this means she therefore needs to live according to the rules and behaviours we expect from anyone else. Just because she has never said to someone *"please stop me when I decide to endanger the lives of others by creating an addictive food craze"* does not mean that we allow her to do it! She has decided that our rules do not apply to her and that her freedom to do is more important than anyone elses!'

Saphia stopped to gather her breath and studied the face in front of her. She could not tell if she was winning or not so she pushed on with her argument.

'Her actions are causing harm. Agreed?'

Cereb nodded his consent.

'You will not act because it would be against her freedoms and because there's nothing written down to say she cannot do this?'

Again, Cereb nodded.

'You know that in reality what she is doing is not only wrong but morally inexcusable?'

Another nod of the head.

'In that case I ask you as a member of our community, who has recognised a harm that is being done, who agrees that it is morally wrong and who has the power to stop this harm to act and to help us using your own right to freedom and your own belief of non-harm."

'I did not catch your name?' asked Cereb.

'Oh sorry. It's Saphia.'

'Well argued Saphia. I am still not completely convinced by your words but I am very disturbed by your pictures. This is a crime against nature and not just a potential harm to our community,' Saphia interrupted him.

'Potential harm!? You haven't seen people to know!'

'You didn't let me finish. People still get to make their own decisions and addictions can be treated. What has been done to the spiders though is something else altogether. It is almost evil. Saphia I am tired. This is as much conversation as I have had in a very long time. Will you leave me with these images? Can you arrange for the others to come back this time tomorrow and we can talk again?'

'Of course. We only came to see if you would even consider helping. To tell the truth Hippy and Yves were pretty sure you wouldn't so any progress is good progress. By tomorrow we should also know if the spiders have been captured.'

Saphia left Cereb, who suddenly seemed quite exhausted, and made her way back down the hallway resisting the urge to open any of the closed doors. When she got outside she found the others were all still there waiting for her return and Vanda had shown up too so she knew the spider collecting had probably begun.

They rushed to her side as soon as she appeared. However, she held her finger up to her lips to ask for silence and made them walk away from the door before she would say anything. When they were a good distance away they stopped.

'What did he say?'

'So did he agree to help?'

'He told you to go away didn't he?'

'I knew it wouldn't work! What will we do now!'

Saphia was bombarded with these and variation of these questions leaving her no space in the conversation to answer them. Instead she took a leaf out of Cereb's book and stayed quiet until they stopped.

'He's kept the pictures and asked us to come back this time tomorrow. I'm not sure I persuaded him but he seemed more bothered by what had been done to the spiders than what had been done to the fairies. For some reason I think he may help us though,' Saphia finally managed to say and before a flood of more questions, all of which would have ended in the same answer, could start she turned to Vanda and asked her a question instead.

'How did you go Vanda?'

'I met Ben. Emma's little brother. He seems a very nice little human. They were about to collect the spiders when I left them and I think they will go back again tomorrow to check they got them all. So mission accomplished. The supply will start drying up and Gula has no way of knowing where her spiders have gone.'

'I cannot believe that Cereb has agreed to help,' said Hippy with a shocked look on his face. 'I really can't believe it.'

Saphia replied 'We don't know if he has yet. He's just asked us to come back tomorrow. Let's not get our hopes up yet,' and she yawned loudly.

'I don't know about the rest of you but these last couple of days have been a bit busy and I think I need to rest up before tomorrow as I suspect it will be even busier. I need my bed and that's where I intend to spend as much time as I can for the rest of the day. I will see you all here tomorrow.'

With that she left them and headed home realising how much energy she had used up. The others watched her go realising that they weren't going to get any more information out of her about Cereb and what had been said in his house. It took the energy out of them too.

101

'Well I have a couple of classes to run before I can rest and if I don't go now I will be late. I will see you all here tomorrow,' said Tattle and off she went too.

The others said their goodbyes, and by now they were all yawning, and went their separate ways wondering what the next day would bring.

"Drink Me"

The next day was greeted by a beautiful sunrise, all pinks, oranges and red with clouds lit up like colourful cotton wool sheep. Tattle was the only one to see it as she was up early to take a gym class. The others, who were all still fast asleep, missed the glorious display.

Sarah had the most disturbed night's sleep as she dreamt of spiders trying to get into pink tutus that Vanda had made for them. They were struggling though because there weren't enough holes in the outfit for their legs. She still remembered it when she woke in the morning and was glad it had been an odd dream rather than a nightmare because even after yesterday she still wasn't confident she would ever like spiders. Sarah wondered what kind of dreams the others had had and ate her breakfast quickly before making her excuses to Aunt Jane, leaving the house, and running up to the farm. When she arrived she found Emma stood on a rung of a gate with her hands and head hanging over the other side looking into a field that had sheep in it. Her little brother Ben was with her.

'I had the weirdest dream last night,' she told them. 'Vanda had made pink tutus for the spiders and they didn't fit.'

Emma replied first, 'I dreamt about winning a gymkhana. There weren't any spiders though.'

Ben shoved his hands deep into his pockets and kicked at pebbles by his feet, 'I don't remember any of my dreams but yours sounds funny to me. Does anyone want to come with me while I go and check for spiders we missed?' he asked.

'We should get that done I guess,' replied Sarah with no enthusiasm for the task at all. 'Then at least it's done and I'll never have to think about them again.'

They got a few more boxes and headed back down to the beck where they had rescued the spiders the day before. The clouds that had made such a pretty sky in the morning had hung around to stay and as they set off it started to drizzle rain on them. This just added to Sarah's lack of enthusiasm for the task but she knew it still needed to be done and she felt responsible for dragging the other two into the fairies business. As it turned out they had done a very good job and there were only a few left to gather. Ben took care to collect some flowers from the hedgerow to take back for the already captured spiders. They looked for fairies that may be guarding the spiders but saw no signs of any. However, it did look like someone had collected the webs that had been left behind.

'I guess that's the last harvest of webs they're going to get. May as well use them rather than let them hang here,' a much more cheerful Sarah remarked knowing that there were fewer spiders to be handled today. 'I wonder what's going on with the fairies now we've taken away their supply? With luck we will find out soon enough. Vanda is bound to show up when there's something to tell us. She can't help it.'

They had just finished settling in the few remaining spiders with the ones they'd got yesterday when exactly that happened. As long as Sarah was carrying the crystal that Vanda had given her then Vanda would always know where she was. Sarah now never left her bedroom without it.

Vanda appeared next to the children in what appeared to be a fancy dress outfit. It was black, slightly fluffy and had long bits sticking out in funny directions.

Sarah burst out laughing and the others joined in. 'What on earth are you wearing?!'

Vanda looked hurt and replied rather sulkily, 'This is something I just threw together. I thought the spiders would be more accepting of me if I made the effort to look like them!'

'It's a spider suit!' shrieked Ben and he started singing the theme tune to the Spiderman show.

'Where are they anyway?' asked Vanda making a show of completely ignoring the giggling and singing.

Ben showed her the containers that he'd set up for the spiders and opened one for her. 'It's quite alright you know. They are perfectly harmless,' he said when he saw how nervous she was.

'Well it's alright for you to say. You're a giant! These things aren't really that much smaller than I am when you think about it.'

The spiders showed no sign of interest in Ben, Vanda or Vanda's outfit. One smaller spider backed off away from her when she approached the container. She followed it from the other side of the clear plastic and eventually it hid under a leaf and she couldn't see it anymore.

'The poor things! It's horrible to think that they have been changed because some awful woman wants to punish us for something we didn't even know we'd done!'

Sarah jumped on this remark. 'Speaking of Gula has anyone seen her since the spiders were taken? Is she angry? What has she been doing? Or has she not even noticed yet?'

'To tell you the truth I haven't given her a second thought since our visit. Some people aren't for changing and Saphia thinks that Gula is one of them. I don't really care what she does. However, I do care what happens to my friends and I even care about these spiders.'

Emma spoke up. 'So what has been happening Vanda? We got the spiders like you asked. Have you spoken to your genius? Is he going to help? Can he change them back again or will we have to hide a mutant group of spiders in this loft forever? Something I know my brother would just love.' She ruffled Ben's hair when she said this and he, in return, thumped her on the arm.

Vanda explained to them what had happened yesterday and how it looked like Saphia had made enough of an impression on Cereb to at least consider helping.

'We are meeting him again this afternoon just like he asked. We can only hope that overnight he's decided to help and that he's got a good idea of what we can do. I'm not sure that you should come along. He doesn't like anyone at all and he only let Saphia into his house yesterday. He seems a very reclusive sort. Please don't be offended but I think yesterday's visit was the only one he's had in a long time and he wasn't happy about it.'

'Everyone is different I guess. We don't need to meet him but please let us know what's happening won't you?' said Emma.

'I will. I hope to have something to share before the end of the day. I'll head off now if that's okay and speak soon.'

She planted her customary kiss on Sarah's forehead and vanished.

'What do we do now?' asked Ben.

'We wait I guess,' replied Emma. 'And we hope she's changed outfit the next time we see her.'

This caused the three of them to collapse into the giggles they'd been holding back when it was clear Vanda had been quite offended by their attitude to her outfit.

The fairies were duly waiting at the allotted time outside Cereb's house. They were all nervous as they still had no backup plan and they weren't feeling that confident on the whole.

Yves, as always though, was the one who was optimistic about their chances. 'I 'ave been thinking 'ard about your talk with 'im Saphia. I believe you persuade 'im. I 'ave to believe it.'

Hippy and Saphia went together to knock on the door while the others held back.

Cereb answered promptly, 'I have been waiting. I was worried you had decided not to come. Come in all of you. Quickly now!' he commanded.

Hippy and Yves stared. This was not the same Cereb they knew. Cereb left the door open and disappeared down the hallway to the kitchen. Saphia, Vanda and Tattle followed him with Yves and Hippy lagging behind. They were confused as to this new development. This was not the Cereb they knew at all.

'I hope you are all well rested and are ready because this is going to be a long day. Since you left I have thought of, and worked on, only this problem,' said Cereb agitatedly. His voice was stronger than the day before. There was a confidence and strength to it that had been absent. He almost seemed excited.

Hippy asked what everyone else was thinking as they all squeezed into the kitchen together. 'This means you will help us?'

'Of course I will help. This thing that has been done is against Nature itself. We cannot tolerate such a blatant misuse of power!' he turned to face Hippy alone. 'This is something I can do that has value Hippy I feel needed now, needed for my abilities. Before I thought I was just needed to fit in and to be what I was expected to be. I pushed that away. I couldn't be like everyone else because I wasn't.'

Hippy looked confused. 'What did you think you were expected to be?'

'I believed people were only interested in me because I was some kind of freak as if I was something to show off and parade. Someone who was wanted only because they were different.'

Hippy took a seat at the table before responding. 'We never wanted that. We wanted you to be happy. We assumed your idea of happiness was the same as our own. One that included family and friends. We wanted to include you that's all. I suppose we wanted you to be like us. I am sorry that we got it so very wrong.'

Cereb looked at him with something approaching pity. 'Well, we can talk about all that later but the clock is ticking and it is against us. I suspect we need to act and act fast. Tell me that you have the spiders?'

Vanda, who had been gazing into a bubbling pot on the stove, responded. 'Yes, our human friends have captured them all and have them contained and looked after. I saw them this morning. The spiders seemed sad.'

Saphia looked askance at her friend. 'Since when did you become an expert in spider psychology? And for that matter since when have you cared?'

'Oh I don't know. I've never really given them much thought really. They seemed sad though, or maybe scared is a better word,' Vanda replied and she reached over to take the top off a jar beside the cooker.

Cereb got there just in time. 'You really don't want to open that. Trust me you don't. So we have the spiders! Well now I need to see one and we need to know how many of them there are. You said they are with humans? How is this possible?'

'It's a long story,' said Vanda with a big sigh. 'But basically Sarah, a human girl, helped us rescue the guests for a birthday party from a grey dragon, then her friend Emma helped us recover a fairy who'd been turned into a wood duck and now Ben, Emma's little brother, is helping us with spiders. They've been very helpful and they are my –sorry our – friends and I trust them.'

'Well I suppose that's good enough for now,' replied Cereb. 'I would perhaps maybe like to hear some more details of the stories you mention later if you'd be so kind. However, first I need to tell you some things and then we need to get a spider to see if I'm right. Please all of you sit.'

While the others found themselves seats around the table Cereb went to a cupboard and got out some mugs which he placed on the table along with the bubbling pot that Vanda had been staring at and a ladle.

'Please help yourselves. It's a recipe of mine I've been refining for quite some time. When I drink it I find I can think clearer and don't get so tired,' Cereb said.

Saphia was brave enough to try it first and then she handed round warm steaming mugs of it to the others. 'It tastes a lot like leek and potato soup!' she exclaimed.

'That's because it is. Mostly. With some extra additions of my own. Nothing harmful I can assure you now drink up.' Cereb took a mug of the soup too and sipped it before he began.

'To begin I will state that in my opinion I believe we are faced with an Alice problem.' He glanced at the blank faces staring back at him and could see he needed to explain a little further. 'Some of you may remember Alice? The rabbit, a Cheshire cat, some teapots and flamingos?'

Yves was confused now, 'Why would Alice 'ave anything to do with spiders? You 'ave mentioned some of the animals. I remember a dormouse too but there were no spiders. Absolutely not.'

'You remember Alice drinking a potion to make her small enough to fit through a door? You remember also that she ate cake to get bigger?'

'Oh yes!' exclaimed Tattle. 'Gosh it's years since I thought about Alice. I wonder where she is now?'

Saphia looked stunned. 'It was a story Tattle. Made up for children. Alice wasn't real you know.'

'Well maybe it was a story and maybe it wasn't,' said Cereb quickly as he could see that the ladies were about to start arguing with each other. 'That's not important right now. You all remember the story though and that's what matters. I strongly suspect that the spiders have been fed the 'eat me' cake. So it is simply a matter of giving them the right amount of 'drink me' potion to reverse the damage.'

There was a moment of stunned silence while they took this in. Vanda was the first to speak up.

'That's it? That's all there is to it? Are you telling me we needed the finest mind in a generation to tell us that? No offence meant of course Cereb,' she said turning to him.

'None taken,' he smiled in reply.

'So all we need to do is get the 'drink me' potion. Right, Saphia where do we get it?'

Saphia looked stunned and perplexed. This wasn't going the way she thought it would. Alice was a story, so everything else was a story too.

'I have no idea do I! And I'm pretty sure it's not something you just go out and get Vanda! I'd bet it's something that's brewed up from a gigantic list of rare and hard to find ingredients!' she said with barely disguised sarcasm.

'Well you changed your tune!' said Tattle with a heavy dose of indignation. 'Just now you were telling me it was a story made up for children!'

'It is just a story!'

'Well it might be mostly story that's true,' interrupted Cereb before it got too heated. 'However, I think you'll find that in every story there is a grain of truth. There are 'eat me' cakes and 'drink me' potions. They just aren't used much these days because, well frankly, they are unreliable. Getting just the right amount is notoriously difficult and, as was the case with Alice, it was much more common to get it quite disastrously wrong. Over time people just stopped using them as there were easier ways to re-size things. In this case though I think the old methods may have been applied because of the length of time they've lasted. Re-sizing living creatures is challenging and most spells wear off quickly. The older potions tended to last much longer and I think that's what's happened given the amount of time the fairy floss has been available now,' explained Cereb.

There was stunned silence in the kitchen. No one really knew if Cereb was having a bit of fun with them or if he was being genuine. Vanda though, always wanting to get the job done and the sooner the better, decided to take advantage of the quiet while the others thought through what Cereb had just said.

'So back to my original question then of where do we get it?' asked Vanda. 'Do you know Cereb? Is it available locally?'

'You can't just go out and buy it I'm afraid. However...' replied Cereb, and here he flourished at them a small book that was well-thumbed and clearly falling apart, '...I have the recipe here in my hand. I will need you all to help me gather the ingredients and we will need a spider to test it on before we give it to them all just to make sure.'

Saphia had now had time to catch up. 'There really are drink me and eat me potions'?'

'Yes. They are not commonly used however, so not surprising you didn't know of them,' replied Cereb kindly.

'There really was an Alice then?' she asked slowly.

'Well there was and there wasn't you see. It's all a bit complicated and we really don't have time for this right now,' he replied.

'See I told you!' exclaimed Tattle triumphantly.

'Will someone explain it to me later please,' Saphia asked weakly. 'I think I need to understand.'

'Of course, I can see your confusion and understand how upsetting that is,' Cereb said to her sympathetically.

Hippy had also had time to think and had mentally made the move right past the discussion about Alice and had caught up to Vanda in wanting to get something done now they seemed to have an answer to the spider issue.

'This is marvellous news!' exclaimed Hippy. 'We can do something! Oh well done Cereb and thank you!'

Yves saw his chance to contribute. 'At Roftmun and Moans we 'ave every ingredient a 'eart could desire. I will get what we need. I propose that Saphia and 'Ippy can 'elp me while I suggest Vanda and Tattle obtain a spider.'

That seemed about it. No one saw a need to argue or discuss further and they all wanted to get on with things so Vanda and Tattle left promptly while Yves took out a notebook and pencil to record the ingredients needed. Yves, Hippy and Saphia then left Cereb in temporary peace while they went to collect the ingredients.

Yves swept into Roftmun and Moans like an avenging angel and started ordering the staff around to collect the items on his list. It was amazing how they listened to everything he said and carefully followed his instructions. Yves didn't ask any one staff member to collect more than two of the items as a precaution.

'You never know. One of them may be in, how you say, cahoots with Gula and 'as been supplying 'er. This way no one will know we are collecting ingredients for a specific potion.'

'That's terribly cunning of you,' said a rather impressed Saphia.

'Ah, it is also good to keep them on their toes,' replied Yves looking rather pleased with himself. 'I will later pretend it was an assessment that contributes to their annual staff review.'

In no time at all they had everything on the list and they returned to Cereb with many bulging bags that were duly emptied out onto the now cleared kitchen table. As they were taken out Cereb ticked them off his list.

'Pineapple. Check. Cherries. Check. Toffee. Check. Eggs. Check. Cream. Check. Butter. Check. Turkey. Check...'

The list went on and on. It was so long that while he recorded the items Saphia had a look at the method of preparation in the book. This would take a while. In fact it would take the rest of the day and some of the evening too. For starters the turkey needed cooking and they had to make custard. The method though was very clear and she turned the oven on and got opening all the cupboards in the kitchen finding the various bowls, spoons, sieves and mashers that would be needed.

Vanda and Tattle didn't think they had time to tell the children about what was going on. They decided together that it was better to wait until they knew that Cereb's hunch was correct before they got them involved. This meant they would have to collect a spider in secret. Vanda luckily knew where the spiders were kept and took Tattle into the loft in the outbuilding of the farm that contained them.

'Oh I'm not sure about this now. I really don't know if I like spiders I'm not sure I'll be able to hold onto one,' said Vanda wringing her hands together in uncertainty.

'Oh don't you worry Vanda. I'll see to this.' Tattle prised the lid off one of the containers with ease. She produced a flower that she had collected along the way and then climbed in amongst the spiders. Again, as they had with Vanda, they showed no interest at all and some even backed away as if they were frightened. Tattle very slowly, and being careful not to make any sudden movements, approached one of the spiders who stared at her. Tattle reached out in front of her with the flower and this seemed to get its attention. With patience she did not realise she had Tattle remained completely still while the spider cautiously felt out the flower with its front legs before crawling its whole body into it to get at the nectar. Tattle held the flower in both arms with the spider cradled within it and backed out of the container quietly.

'It's heavier than it looks,' she said as she got back to her friend. 'Unless you want to hold it, and I doubt you do, you'll have to close that box back up for me Vanda.'

Vanda hurriedly managed to force the container lid back down again and the two of them, with their captive spider, made their way back to Cereb's house. Once they were there the preparations were in full swing for the 'drink me' potion. Cereb had created an efficient, well drilled team of assistants out of Hippy, Saphia and Yves. Together they moved around the kitchen without getting in each other's way. Noise was kept to a minimum as Cereb was so used to being alone and working alone it was the only way he could think.

The team worked quietly all day and well into the evening stopping to drink Cereb's potato and leek soup when they felt the need for a little more energy and focus. As the instructions progressed they became more difficult and exacting and Cereb began to micromanage every small step of the process to ensure they got it perfectly right. No one minded as they didn't want to get it wrong because it would mean starting all over again. They were a team with a clear purpose and Cereb expected them to work at, or beyond their abilities even, and none of them wanted to disappoint him when he'd placed so much trust in them.

'We are nearly there everyone,' said a gently perspiring Cereb. The kitchen had become quite warm with them all in it and with all the burners of the stove in use. 'We need to be careful we get exactly the right amount of each of the preparations otherwise who knows what we'll make.'

Cereb took control, and the others happily let him, when it came to the final combination.

'Thirteen drops of this into seventeen drops of that green one. Stir anti clockwise and then pour gently into the dark red juice over a low flame. After five minutes take off the heat and add two tablespoons of custard...' Cereb carefully followed the instructions while the rest kept a hushed silence while they watched. Saphia stood close to the book and cross checked everything Cereb was doing as he went along whispering along and nodding her head as each step was completed.

Finally it was over. The kitchen was piled high with bowls and beakers, spoons and sieves that all needed cleaning but they were all too exhausted to do it. They sat silently round the table gazing at a cooling container of liquid that steamed gently. Yves was already nodding off to sleep where he sat when he was disturbed by Cereb.

'I think it is cool enough now to try,' he said removing a thermometer from the beaker in front of them.

Tattle went to fetch the spider than had been left in another room hidden in its flower all day.

'Given the size of the spider and taking into account how fresh this potion is I think we must start on only a drop and work up from there if we need to.

'How big is a drop anyway?' asked Vanda.

'This big,' replied Cereb as he produced a small set of spoons of different sizes held together as if they were a bunch of keys. He selected the smallest spoon and showed it to her before measuring out exactly one drop of the potion. This he proffered to the spider who had retreated into its flower as far as it could go.

Thankfully, the potion was mostly made of a lot of sweet things. The sugariness was sensed by the spider who began drinking the liquid in the spoon that had been balanced carefully on a petal of the flower.

They didn't have to wait long for something to happen. As the spider drank they saw it shrinking before their eyes. One drop it seemed was enough to do the job. The spider was now a small little thing maybe ten times smaller than it had been just a moment ago.

Cereb produced another notebook and took a measuring tape out of one of the many pockets in his jacket. He measured the length of the spider and checked it against a life size image of the same spider he had in the book.

'I am happy to tell you that we have succeeded!' he said. 'This spider is now its normal size. You can all be very proud of yourselves!'

The team were too tired to do anything other than grin at each other across the table. None of them had the energy to celebrate.

'I've never worked so hard, or concentrated so hard, before,' said Vanda. 'I'm happy, so happy but completely exhausted.'

'Well we know we have the answer now,' said Cereb. 'I was right first time. I think some rest is in order for us all and then we need to take this beaker to the other spiders and hope that it is enough to treat all of them otherwise we'll have to make up another batch.'

The others mumbled their exhausted agreement with Cereb. Now that they had sat down their beds were the only thing any of them could think of. They tiredly got back to their feet and said their goodbyes to Cereb. As they left, with Tattle taking the now much reduced but apparently happier spider with her in the flower, they agreed to meet in the morning. Then they would let the children know what they'd done and get on with fixing the other spiders.

Shrinking spiders, Racing Round and Gula's gone

As agreed the fairies met, after a very good night's sleep, early in the morning. They were a lot happier and more enthusiastic about their achievement of the day before after a few hours in bed. Vanda was sent to find the children and luckily Ben, Emma and Sarah were all together in the first place she looked at the farm.

'Stay right where you are! We have a lot to tell you!' she shouted before vanishing.

They didn't have to wait long before she reappeared with the rest of the fairies including one they hadn't met before who was carefully carrying a large container full of a dark red liquid.

'First can we go to the spiders and get started and we can explain on the way?' said Vanda taking charge of the situation. The rather odd little group headed to the outbuilding loft where the spiders were being kept and, while they went, the fairies got the children up to speed with the progress they had made in the last day.

Let me get this right. There really is a 'drink me' potion like the one in the Alice story? And you made it? And it's the antidote to the 'eat me' cake that Gula has fed the spiders?' said a somewhat amazed Emma. 'I really am living in a story now.'

'Cool,' said Ben. 'I reckon it's pretty bonkers but guess we'd better get started.'

Cereb (who refused to be introduced to the humans and seemed less confident and more detached now that the problem had been solved) began to carefully measure out drops of the liquid into spoons they had brought with them. Not all the spoons being used were the same size but they all received a measure from the same one drop spoon he had used the day before. As Cereb measured out Ben opened the containers so that each spider could get a drop of 'drink me' potion.

It took a little while as they had to wait for each spider to finish their drop before they could move on to feeding it to another but it was fascinating to watch the spiders shrink. Even Sarah was

116

amazed to see the change and quite overcame her fear of them once they were back to their normal size. Tattle, who had remembered to bring the spider that had been used to test the potion, reunited it with the others in the box it had been in once they had all shrunk in size. She had been worried that the smaller spider would be intimidated by all the bigger ones.

'They seem so much happier,' said Vanda. 'I think they knew that something bad had been done to them and that's why they seemed so sad before.'

'What do we do with them now though?' asked Ben. 'It's not like we can take them back where we found them. If that crazy fairy is still around she'll just do it again won't she?'

Saphia answered, 'We will just have to find a different place to free them. These spiders don't normally stay in the same place for long so not taking them back isn't a problem. If there's another beck close by that should do just fine.'

They all agreed that the now much reduced spiders could be left with the children and they would find a good place to free them that was nowhere near the place they'd been captured.

'I have to say I am very impressed at how quickly you've made all this happen and come up with an answer,' said Sarah trying to get Cereb to engage with them. 'How did you solve it?'

This was not a question any of the others had asked him. They'd been so busy just getting the job done once he agreed they hadn't had time to think of asking.

Cereb however said nothing audible and simply mumbled something into his beard. He was definitely not telling anyone how he'd worked it out today.

Sarah was undeterred and carried on, 'Well I think it's brilliant anyway even if you don't want to share how it was done with us. Congratulations.'

Vanda was the one to disturb their good mood. 'We still may have a problem. Gula's supply will be drying up and that big warehouse of fairy floss will start to empty. I'm not sure she'll be happy about that at all. Remember she showed no signs of caring at all about the consequences of her actions when we met her Saphia. I wonder what she'll do?'

Saphia shook her head, 'I have no idea. It's not like we spent enough time with her to get to know any likely action she'd take. She wasn't one for sharing. However, I'm going to guess that she'll just disappear the same way she suddenly appeared but who knows?'

The little group discussed the likely action of Gula quietly amongst themselves while Cereb and Ben continued to feed the spiders the 'drink me' potion. The conversation unfortunately kept going round in circles and they came up with sillier and sillier ideas about how she'd go mad, or how she'd just go, or how she'd take revenge. They were really just filling time. No idea was any better than any other as to what might happen.

Eventually, all the spiders had received their dose of the potion and it was time for Ben, Emma and Sarah to take them to a new home. The fairies left them to it, with Cereb still not saying a word, but Vanda promised they would tell them what happened to Gula as soon as they knew.

As it turned out after two more days it became clear that Gula had in fact simply gone. The supplies of fairy floss got smaller and smaller and more and more expensive until there was none left.

Vanda and Saphia made the decision to return to the big warehouse where they'd gone pretending to be Roftmun and Moans employees. There they found the same fairy, Size, who had been there last time and asked him what had happened.

'Well I guess the spiders have finally gone on somewhere else like they always do. I reckon we'll never see such a big crop as that in my lifetime and maybe in you young 'uns neither. That's all fine by me mind. It's way past time for our holiday to Cornwall as it is. The wife's been itching to go these past two weeks. Just the last few bags left now, and they're only small ones and right expensive too I can tell you.'

Saphia and Vanda then went to the house that they had met Gula in and spent a while knocking on the door. When no one came they spent some time peering in through the windows. When that didn't reveal anything either they tried the door handles and window frames to see if they were locked. They were. It seemed that Gula had just upped and gone when it was clear her fairy floss business was over.

Saphia struggled with this even though she had said it had been the most likely outcome. 'It just doesn't make sense though! She was very, very sure of herself when we saw her. I expected her to put up some kind of fight. Instead there have been no accusations, no appeals and no crazy behaviour. She didn't really seem the type to up and leave.'

'I agree,' said Vanda sitting with her friend staring at the front door that remained firmly shut to them. 'I thought she'd fight, or get angry or do something wild. To just disappear doesn't make sense. All that planning all that revenge that had been built over the years can't have just vanished can it?'

'Probably not. Maybe there was no backup plan? Maybe she thinks that what she has done is enough. We may never know. We do know that she is still out there and certainly doesn't like us anymore today than she did a month ago. We may not have seen the last of her. This defeat may just stoke the fires of revenge even more.'

'Well I don't love that particularly optimistic outlook Saphie dear,' sighed Vanda. I hadn't thought that that by solving one problem we could be making another. Come on,' she said standing up indicating she was ready to go, 'we promised Tattle we'd meet her at the gym and if we don't go now we'll be late.'

119

When they got to the gym it seemed like everyone else was there too and it also looked like all the equipment that had been inside had been brought outside.

In the centre of a crowd they could see the energetic figure of Tattle cheering and yelling.

'Woo hoo! Alright that must be a new PB for Keta there! She's absolutely smashing this course up. I'm not sure anyone will be able to beat that!' Tattle's exclamation marks were back. After nearly a week of her being tired, fed up, exhausted and beaten this was the girl they knew and loved.

'What on earth is going on?' shouted Saphia above the din as they managed to fight their way in to Tattle's side. 'What are all these people doing?'

Tattle turned to her friends with a beaming smile, 'It's just awesome don't you think!?'

'We guess so but what is it exactly?' Saphia tried again.

'It's Racing Round! Remember! That event that no one did at the Highland Games and Hippy was happy because if they had done he thought it would have killed someone?! Well they're doing it! Too many people signed up to run it indoors so we had to take it outside! Some of the competitors got a real shock at the games and started to take their exercise seriously. Probably even more seriously than they did before the Highland Games. Some of them have got really, really fit and I'm so proud of them all!'

Tattle dragged Vanda and Saphia away from the melee of bodies so they didn't have to shout.

'A day ago I decided that some of them had done so well they needed a new challenge so I brought Racing Round back! It seems like not just a few people were interested, it seems like everyone was up for it, and so we've had to bring the competition outside and it's just fabulous don't you think?! People have brought extra friends and then word seems to be travelling fast and even more people are arriving! This is going to go on all day!'

Tattle was grinning from ear to ear and her explanation was interspersed with people giving her high fives and shouting 'woo hoo!' and 'we've so got this' a lot.

'Ah ha! There you are!' Sivle appeared by the ladies wearing his gym kit. 'Isn't this fun! I'd forgotten how much fun working out can be!'

'Oh my,' whispered Saphia to Vanda. 'It seems this enthusiasm is catching.'

'Are you two taking part too? Everyone else seems to be so you might as well. I can explain the course to you if you like?' he turned to address Tattle alone for a second. 'Tattle you're wanted back in the middle. It seems Keta and Jerip are arguing about proper form on the large wall. It could get ugly.'

Tattle dashed off away from them and into the crowd. Meanwhile Sivle, who it must be said looked a lot healthier than he had a week ago, dragged Vanda and Saphia round the edge of the crowd to where the start of the course began. Once there he tried his best to explain how it worked. He had to shout over the absolute mayhem going on around him though. There's nothing like a herd of fairies for noise. You have to hear it to believe it.

'So you start here with the crawling under the ivy section and then it's up the small wall and down to the area where you do squats then push ups then star jumps and a plank sequence – I can show you that later – you see where Tattle is? Well the course carries on there through a pool of water and you have to hold your breath before the upper body weights section, you can see there are three different stations, the pull ups are my personal favourite, then it's a dash over the balance beams and onto the lower body weights and finally you go over the large wall and swing across that finishing line by Hippy. Tattle's decided there are prizes for fastest and also who can do the most repetitions before exhaustion! I tell you it's her best workout ever!'

'I feel exhausted just looking at it,' said Saphia.

'I don't know,' said Vanda. 'I'm just going to get changed I'll be back in a tick. This looks fun!'

'You don't need to wait for me Sivle, off you go again. I'll go and chat to Hippy.'

Sivle wandered off and Saphia fought her way across to Hippy on the finish line.

'So there's no fairy floss anymore but we seem to have a lot of exercise happening. I guess that's good then isn't it?' she said to him crossing her arms and doing her best to keep out of the way of the enthusiasm all around her.

'Well I suppose so. This seems quite an extreme sort of event though. I came along just in case something happened. It is much more strenuous than anything we normally do. So far so good though; nothing of note has happened to anyone yet. I should say that there is a marked improvement in the overall appearance of a lot of them and they do seem happier.'

He was about to continue when a high pitched cry of anguish came from the large wall. Looking over they could see a fairy crumpled at the bottom of it with an agonised expression on her face clutching at her shoulder.

'It seems I spoke too soon. Please excuse me Saphia I think I may have some work to do after all.'

Hippy made his way over to the wall and took charge of the situation gently leading the injured party away from the course. He supported the fairy as best he could who was whimpering in pain but also trying to look like the injury was nothing at all. There was polite applause as she was lead away and then things quickly got back to the race.

Saphia watched on in amusement, there seemed to be multiple people on the course at all times, and the bystanders were generous in their support and also their advice. This meant it was absolute bedlam and the noise level just seemed to keep going up and up. She stayed long enough to see Vanda reappear, as promised, in her gym gear and then headed home to leave them all to their fun as she didn't feel like giving it a go today. She could watch them compete from a window in her home anyway as she lived very close by.

When she got there she found on her doorstep a huge bouquet of flowers. She first looked around to see if there was anyone around and then bent down to pick out a card she could see peeking out of the corner of the wrapping. She was surprised to see it had her name on it. Her initial thought had been they had been delivered to the wrong house as she had never been given flowers before.

She quickly picked up the bouquet and went inside. First she placed the flowers in a vase of water and then she opened the card and read the words inside.

'To Saphia. I hope you will accept these as a token of my friendship, Yves.'

Saphia didn't know what to think! Her brain ran wild with disorganised thoughts that she was uncomfortable with. She tried unsuccessfully to distract herself watching the Racing Round from her window.

By early evening the noise level around the gym started dropping off. Keta did win the overall fastest time and was rewarded with free gym classes for the rest of the year. Looking out of her window at the tired but happy competitors Saphia saw that Ignis and Saltyp, who had put on the fire lights and bangs display on at the Highland Games, had taken advantage of the large gathering to put on another display of their bright coloured sparkles and bangs. She had to admit it was quite impressive with a finale of a huge rainbow that travelled from left to right across the sky finishing just where Tattle stood. Then the crowds started to disperse and head home as the day's activities caught up with them. Saphia caught sight of Vanda as she came past and called out to her.

'How did you go? Was it fun?'

'Truthfully I think I maybe wasn't fit enough for it but I will be next time. Tattle has plans to turn it into some kind of monthly event. With teams too! You can be on mine if you like?' replied Vanda.

'Hmm I'll have a think about it if you don't mind and get back to you tomorrow. By the way when you got home earlier was there anything waiting for you? And talking of tomorrow we should go and see the children and let them know about Gula and find out where they put the spiders.'

Vanda replied, 'No nothing at all at mine and you're right we should talk to Sarah and Emma.'

And before Saphia could tell Vanda about the flowers she was already waving at her as she continued past the house. 'I'll see you here at nine tomorrow morning.'

Saphia tried to take her mind off the flowers and went to bed early with a book to calm her brain down.

Apparently no one won the most repetitions before exhaustion event as there were still three people on course when everyone else had gone home.

In the morning Vanda and Saphia met at nine and then popped over to see the children who were playing with the farm dogs. They explained that Gula had simply up and left after the spiders had been taken and they told them about the new exercise craze that Tattle had started.

'And look here,' said Vanda brandishing a tiny magazine. 'The Fabulous Fairy is back to normal! I picked this up first thing this morning it's the latest edition. There are no adverts or recipes for fairy floss to be found anywhere, I've checked. Can you believe it!'

Together the little group congratulated each other on their success over the last few days. Ben was almost disappointed that it was all over and there was no baddy to chase or catch.

'We took the spiders somewhere else to release them. I'm sure they've moved on already so there's no point in showing you I guess,' Ben said. 'So what happens now?'

'Oh I don't know but I reckon we should start with finding out who Saphia's admirer is!' replied Vanda.

On the way to see them Saphia had told Vanda that she had received flowers. She hadn't told her, because she was still quite confused about it, that they had come from Yves.

'Cut it out!' Saphia said defensively.

'What do you mean? You have an admirer Saphia?' asked Emma.

Saphia crossed her arms and looked quite unwilling to discuss the matter. 'I got some flowers yesterday that's all. Just flowers. Nothing to get excited about. Now can we just change the subject please.'

'I guess there's no need for us to be hanging out anymore now. Spiders fixed and mysterious evil fairy vanished and everything?' asked a very disappointed Ben.

'Well if the last couple of weeks is anything to go by I would say enjoy the rest while you can,' replied his big sister Emma. 'With these fairies something is always about to happen it's just a matter of time before they'll be showing up on our doorstep again asking us to help stop the fire-breathing dragon or the plague of chocolate snowmen!'

'She's right you know,' said Sarah. 'Give them a day or two and it'll be onto the next puzzle, or mystery, and then they'll be needing their friends us humans to help them out.'

'We just like making your otherwise dull lives more interesting!' replied Vanda.

'And it's quite fun having human friends. You're different to us,' added Saphia.

And with that they parted company knowing that it probably wouldn't be long before they needed each other again.

THE END